Other Burlap Hall Mysteries

Phantom of Burlap Hall
Poltergeist of Burlap Hall
Vampire Master of Burlap Hall

SPACEBOY
AT
BURLAP HALL

VIRGINIA IRONSIDE

WALKER BOOKS
AND SUBSIDIARIES
LONDON · BOSTON · SYDNEY

First published 1989 by Walker Books Ltd
87 Vauxhall Walk, London SE11 5HJ

2 4 6 8 10 9 7 5 3 1

This edition published 1997

Text © 1989 Virginia Ironside
Cover illustration © 1997 Jeff Cummins

This book has been typeset in Sabon.

Printed in England

British Library Cataloguing in Publication Data
A catalogue record for this book is available
from the British Library.

ISBN 0-7445-5409-8

For
Ruth Grove-White

CHAPTER ONE

At the sound of a van revving up in the driveway of Burlap Hall, Mr Fox, the headmaster, leapt to his study window. Surely, he thought, the builders could hardly be packing in their first day's work! It was only two o'clock! He leant out to give them a shout, but their van was already roaring off round the corner. Then a great splat of rain hit the top of his balding head. So that was what had driven them away. A teensy weensy little drop of rain! Shocking! But when a gust of threatening wind swirled into the room (dislodging the few hairs that Mr Fox had carefully scraped over his scalp, in an effort to look less bald) he shut the window. The light faded. A summer storm was brewing. With a sigh, he sat down and turned back to the papers on his desk.

Bad news and more bad news – unpaid bills; a letter from a parent explaining that he was sending his daughter to the rival St Beowulf's rather than Burlap Hall because Burlap Hall was "far too old-fashioned"; a card from Mr Fritz, the science teacher, enclosing a doctor's note insisting that he have a total rest from work for a term. And, worst of all, a letter from Clive Nutter, the Schools' Inspector from the Lanchestershire Education Department.

For the fiftieth time since he'd received it in the Easter holidays, Mr Fox picked it up.

"Dear Mr Fox," it read, "I am sorry to have to tell you" ("Sorry!" scoffed Mr Fox) "that under Clause One, sub-section three, footnote b(iii), that science studies must form an integral part of the syllabus and

7

facilities must be in compliance with sub-section H(2).

Unless this situation is rectified within the aforesaid time-limit (see Building Regs BS341) the school may have to be closed down in accordance with sub-section 6 of Section 2 of sub-section H iii.

I am therefore giving you notice of my forthcoming visit to inspect the school, not only to ensure that you are taking urgent steps to update your science facilities but also to check that the educational standards of the school are of at least the minimum levels required by my education department.

Yours sincerely,

Clive Nutter

Clive Nutter, Schools' Inspector,
Lanchestershire County Council"

In other words – "build a new science block or else you'll be out of a job."

This was why plans had been hastily drawn up and that very morning, the second week of term, builders had arrived to lay the foundations of the building that would, in time, be the new science block. But when would "in time" be? And where would the money come from? No parents had so far responded to Mr Fox's letter begging for donations to the new building.

True, the school was rather curling at the edges; damp was coming through the walls, the heating constantly broke down, most of the textbooks had been published well before 1920 and the maps on the walls still showed Britain as ruling half the countries in the world. But so far they'd somehow muddled through.

And what was the point of all these new-fangled machines and gadgets, anyway? They drove Mr Fox mad. He didn't know a fax from a modem or a satellite dish from a casserole dish.

Gloomily, he stared at his dusty, glass-fronted cabinets which contained ancient copies of the *Encyclopaedia Britannica* (Vols Sc–Sy and Do–Du missing, no doubt due to the fact that they contained the sections "Sex" and "Drugs") and pondered on the situation.

Clive Nutter! Nutter was his arch enemy from twenty years ago, when they had both applied for the headmastership of Burlap Hall. He recalled, with acute distaste, the sight of Nutter's cunning, beady eyes, his breath that smelt of old cabbage, his bony figure and gnarled knuckles, his pale, grey skin and his short, mousy hair smarmed back over a domed, greasy, white forehead. His voice, he remembered, was a horrible, high-pitched, bitter whine that reeked of punishment and revenge.

And Nutter had never forgiven Mr Fox for getting the job. Once he became the local Schools' Inspector, he'd made it his business to try to oust Mr Fox from his post.

Nutter had sprung food inspectors on him from nowhere, forcing him to close down the kitchens, on the grounds that they were unhygienic – meaning Mr Fox had had to spend a fortune on refurbishing them. Then he'd claimed that the medical facilities were unacceptable – resulting in more expense. And now Mr Fox had to gear himself for another visit from the frightful Nutter. Minimum standards, indeed! What cheek!

In the meantime, as a sop to the Lanchestershire

Education Department and in the absence of Mr Fritz, the science teacher, Mr Carstairs, who taught English, was preparing what he called the "now" generation for their first step into the twentieth century – with a Computer Studies course.

And that was how it came about that Tom Buxton (who, although fourteen, didn't feel remotely like a member of the "now" generation) found himself that evening with his friends, Miles and Susan, wrestling over the impossible Computer Studies prep set for the class by Mr Carstairs.

The three of them sat gloomily in the Computer Room. It was actually just the Nature Studies Room with a new name on the door; on the walls were still pinned pieces of paper entitled "Seed Distribution" with burs and sycamore seeds and dusty dandelion heads glued on to them. Someone had done a tracing of a great spotted woodpecker on another sheet and, dangling underneath at an angle and missing a drawing pin, was a picture that looked like a bull's-eye but was in fact a cross-section of a tree, showing the number of years it had lived.

Tom felt he knew that great spotted woodpecker personally, so often had his eyes strayed from the baffling signs on the computer screen to rest on its lividly dappled chest. And all the time the summer storm was still dithering about when and where to break. The rain outside hammered on the roof while the green screens of the computers flickered mockingly in front of them.

The problems he was having were compounded by the fact that all adults seemed to think that anyone under the age of sixteen could take to computers like a duck to water. Even his father had said, "Oh, *I* could never understand computers in a million years, but you'll have no problems because you're young and the younger generation doesn't suffer from techno-fear."

It wasn't so much techno-fear that Tom suffered from. It was techno-rage. The wretched computer *would* keep answering back.

He'd type in some extremely simple command and the computer would reply, like a total der-brain, "?"

Finally he typed, in a fury, "Ax2disk you great fool!" and the computer just replied, "Ax2disk you great fool!" followed by, "?"

It was enough to make you cry.

Mr Carstairs had asked the class to explain the "generation of the bit image data" by using examples. But every time Tom tried he either got the usual "?" message or a series of incomprehensible remarks like "Baud rate cannot be set for this device" or "Invalid HEX digit".

To make matters worse flashes of lightning ripped now across the windows, illuminating the whole room with eerie silver streaks; an instant later, thunder crashed, showing that the storm was hovering just above.

"Do you understand any of this?" asked Miles, finally, looking up. He was Tom's best friend, a year older and with braces on his teeth. His father was a doctor and extremely rich and he'd always rather annoyed Tom with his descriptions of the gadgets that filled their home – including word processors, computers and X-ray machines. But his electronic home-life seemed to have had no effect on his grasp of how the things worked.

Then Susan spoke. "I thought I'd mastered – I mean

11

mistressed – the basic principles when Carstairs was explaining it to me, but it sure isn't so easy putting it into practice." She sat looking baffled at her machine. In the low light, her face and wild, frizzy red hair lit up only by the green screen, she looked almost supernatural.

"Maybe it's this storm," said Miles, shivering slightly as the rain rattled at the windows. "Maybe the electrical currents are interfering with the interface."

"Or they're interfacing with the interfere," said Tom. "I don't know an interface from a modem."

"Don't call me madam," said Susan, automatically. Susan was originally from Los Angeles but had ended up at Burlap Hall because her parents were diplomats at the American Embassy in Rome. Susan's mother had burnt her bra during some happening in the sixties and her daughter was anxious to carry on the family's feminist tradition. Never "praying mantis", always "praying womantis"; never "Manchester United" but always "Personchester United". When they'd once organized a debate and Susan was elected Chairman, she insisted on being called "Chair" instead. Miles, who secretly fancied Susan, had tried to sit on her, much to everyone's amusement.

At his desk, Miles stretched and put his hand to his head. "I'm bored," he said. "Who cares about computers? Let's tell Carstairs we don't understand any of it so he'll just have to explain it to us again."

Susan switched off her machine and got up. "He can stick his wretched bits and bytes up his jumper for all I care. Come on," she added to Tom as she passed by his desk, "give up. Admit it. You're defeated."

Tom hesitated. Just at that moment and for the first time he felt he had the idea nearly in his grasp – and it was worth a final attempt. It wasn't so much that he didn't understand the computer; it was more that the computer didn't understand him. If only, he thought, computers could be taught "Human Studies"; then they might not give such footling replies.

"I'll be up in a minute," he said. "I just want to have one more go."

"You're a glutton for punishment," said Miles, as he and Susan left. He made a ghastly face at him by pulling his mouth out at the sides with his fingers. "You'll turn into one of those computer boffins if you don't watch out. All glasses and mad hair and plastic shoes."

And they left him with the computers, the empty desks and the rain for company.

It was lonely in that great big room. Being in an empty classroom always gave Tom a funny feeling. The fact that there were so many unfilled chairs emphasized the absence of other pupils. There was no sound but the beating of the rain, the occasional squeak of the computer when he made a mistake, the creak of the old floorboards and suppressed giggles outside in the corridor as pupils passed the room on the way to their dormitories.

Tom tried his proposition again.

"Ax2disk" he typed, hopefully. No luck. The computer simply did its old trick and flashed up, "?"

In a fit of fury he slammed both his hands on to the computer keyboard – and at exactly the same time an enormous crack of thunder nearly burst Tom's eardrums. A blade of lightning streaked right into the room and Tom closed his eyes tightly. All around the thunder cracked and spluttered so loudly that Tom instinctively put his hands over his head in case the ceiling fell on him; the explosive flash from the lightning had left him with green spots in front of his eyes when he opened them again. His ears hummed and his brain buzzed. Slowly the thunder rumbled away, like a giant rolling huge stones over distant hills, and Tom turned to look again at the computer.

But something had happened. There, on the screen, was a message which read, "Can I help you?"

Tom blinked. Could this really be the same computer that he'd been struggling with for the last half-hour? Surely not. He stared again, then carefully typed in, "Yes, please." He felt a bit creepy. Surely this wasn't meant to happen?

"Request question, please," replied the computer.

Tom paused. The computer had never asked him for a question before. Then, with a little shrug, he typed, "I want to know why, when I type in 'Ax2disk', you reply with a question mark."

The computer buzzed a little. "Press Enter after message, for required computer reply," it responded.

"But I thought you *were* the computer," typed Tom, surprised.

"No discussion, please," replied the computer.

Tom continued with his homework and finally, much to his astonishment, the answer was explained brilliantly from start to finish on a spotless printout. It was completely uncanny. He stared at the screen and then at the printout and even peered around the back of the computer – but he could find nothing that would account for its strange behaviour.

Shaking slightly, Tom was just about to turn the computer off when another message flashed on to the screen, "Please return favour for help given." This was all utterly extraordinary. He'd never had a conversation with a computer before.

"What do you want me to do?" he typed.

On the computer screen came various instructions about which buttons Tom was to press; he dutifully followed its requests. Finally it came up with, "At next flash of lightning, press Y."

Tom waited. And waited. The rain continued to patter down but the storm seemed to be getting further and further away. Only distant rumbles of thunder burped through the sky like an old man who'd eaten too much at dinner. Then, just as he was about to give up, a flashing knife of lightning, even bigger than the last, burst through the window. Its jagged edges seemed to singe the desks and its fiery point stabbed into the floor with an almighty crack. Simultaneously the thunder built up and up, in a mighty crescendo so loud that the very room shivered with the sound. The windows almost burst open and the desks rattled on the floor. Tom hastily checked to see where Y was and then, keeping his eyes tightly shut, pressed it.

As the thunder faded away, he found himself in pitch darkness. The lights had fused and the computer lay dead in front of him, its screen black as a blind man's glasses.

Far away he could hear other people in the school shouting as they looked for lights. He got up, feeling for the computer printout, and made his way slowly to the door.

What an absolutely weird experience! Even though he was elated at having completed the prep, he felt curiously wobbly and trembly, as if he'd strayed into strange territory. He must get a grip on himself. He reached for the door knob. Then he stopped. There was a noise. A noise that was in the same room. It was a kind of … a kind of giggling sound.

15

"Miles?" he said, into the blackness.

No answer.

"Susan?"

Nothing.

Then suddenly something cold and fleshy bumped into him. It was like being slapped by a dead fish or pressed up against a lizard. Whatever it was it felt too cold to be alive; there again, it certainly wasn't dead. Tom groped desperately at the door handle but whatever it was had reached it first. Tom's hand brushed against a piece of scaly flesh. He felt the door opening and something rushed by him with a cold gust of air, brushing softly past his legs. Then whatever it was scampered out into the corridor.

Tom stood, frozen with fear, staring into the darkness. He was so frightened that for a few minutes he forgot to breathe; then his lungs started to work again and his breath came back, panting from him in quick terrified gasps. He couldn't make anything out at all in the darkness. But there was definitely something there. He could hear it giggling. And then he heard the sharp sound of footsteps on the corridor floor getting fainter and fainter.

But they weren't ordinary footsteps. They had a hard tapping sound, like the footsteps of an animal; an animal with long claws.

CHAPTER TWO

As the early morning sun filtered into the bedroom he shared with Miles, Tom woke distinctly uneasy. His sleep had been plagued with nightmares; his head was full of worry and dark scenes and disturbing emotions. And yet now he couldn't recall any of them.

Then he remembered the extraordinary events of the night before, the thunderstorm, the computer speaking to him – and, worst of all, the awful giggling sound and the distinct memory of cold, clammy, almost inhuman flesh bumping into him. It was bad enough being at boarding school at all; he never slept as well there as he did at home. (However many posters he and Miles put up, the dingy, brown curtains, the horrible woodchip wallpaper, the worn carpet and the patches of damp on the walls still dominated the room, giving it an unmistakably institutional stamp.) But the memory of the night before had made what was barely tolerable even less tolerable. Just the thought of that giggle made Tom go all goose-pimply and he pulled his bedclothes round him, turning his Walkman on quietly to dispel the creepy feelings. It was nice to hear the soothing sounds of rap music; it made everything seem more normal.

Then Miles' voice broke into his thoughts.

"So when did you get to sleep last night? I didn't hear you come in." Miles was starting to wake up, rubbing his eyes. Tom could hear him stretching in the bed beside him.

"About midnight, I suppose," said Tom, unhooking one of his ear-pieces. "I had this horrible sort of ..."

"Bet you didn't get the homework done," interrupted Miles, turning to him and smiling in the half-light of the early morning.

"Well, I did, actually," Tom replied. "It was really uncanny. You see there was this flash of thund—"

"Where? How did you do it?" Miles looked around the room and, seeing a pile of papers on the table, hopped out of bed and glanced at Tom's homework. He grabbed his dressing-gown and tied it around himself. He pulled open one of the curtains and started to read the printout.

"Amazing! I don't understand a word of it!" he said. "But it all works out in the end, doesn't it? Are you sure you did this yourself?" He came over to Tom and ruffled his hair. "Funny, your brain seems the same size as it did yesterday."

"In other words, bigger than yours," said Tom.

"Can I copy it?" said Miles.

"I'm just worried," said Tom. "You see, I don't really understand it myself. What happened was ..."

"Oh, go on. After all, I let you have my history notes. And I did that geometry problem for you ..."

"It's not that," said Tom, getting out of bed. "It's just that you don't understand. It was so unusual."

"Certainly unusual for you to be able to do any computer homework," said Miles, sitting down, pulling some paper towards him and starting to copy it. "Actually," he added as he got under way, "it's quite interesting."

But Tom had gone to have a wash and was no longer in the room.

In the communal bathroom a gaggle of boys was tittering and laughing. Some were flicking each other with wet flannels, others were making towels into turbans and dancing round pretending to be Egyptians, while the soap was flying into the air, being hidden behind the taps, wrestled over and squeezed out of people's hands so that it leapt to the ceiling like a rocket.

Tom found a basin next to Simon who was chatting to Asquith Minor. Asquith Major had left Burlap Hall years ago but his younger brother was still saddled with "Minor", a title he daily tried to disprove.

"He's got this really thin body," Asquith Minor was saying. "And his face looks kind of green."

"I don't think he blinks," said Simon. "And his hair is all wispy."

"And have you seen the clothes he wears?" said Asquith Minor. "Buttoned up to his neck even in summer – and woolly gloves as well."

"Who's this?" asked Tom, undoing his pyjama top to have a wash.

"The new boy," said Asquith Minor. He was drying his face and his voice was muffled through a towel. "Arrived this morning. He's really weird."

"He probably can't help it," said Tom, kindly, punching the tap before he whipped his hands under the brief gush of water that spurted out. You had to be incredibly nifty to get the hot water out of the taps at Burlap Hall this term because over the holidays Mr Fox had had them fixed in such a way that great skill was needed to get your hands under the water before it cut off again. It was yet another means of saving on the bills. "Simon – will you push while I wash?"

Simon leant over and pressed the tap.

"They say his parents are very rich," he said. "And that's why Mr Fox has let him come to school a week late."

19

"Not fair," said Asquith Minor.

"Jolly not," said Simon.

Meanwhile Mr Fox was still in bed, mulling over an odd incident he'd experienced the night before. He'd returned from the Stoat and Otter soaking wet, caught in the storm both on the way there and on the way back. As he had pushed open the doors of Burlap Hall raindrops plopped off the end of his nose. Everything was normal when he returned: the sounds of Signor Ruzzi, the music teacher, snoring in his bedroom; the same old holes in the stained and balding carpets – all the more in evidence since the lampshade had fallen off the central light on the half-landing, leaving a hideously exposed bare bulb; there were the same number of stair-rods missing – he *must* do something about them, he resolved for the hundredth time, or a pupil would slip and get hurt. And Mr Fox just tried to forget that he'd been unable to afford to renew the insurance for the pupils this term. There was the same sharp smell of boiled cabbage, disinfectant, sweat and sharpened pencils lingering in the air – and the window on the landing was *still* cracked from last term, when a boy had kicked a football at it. A large sphere of polished wood wobbled dangerously on the corner banister; soon that would break off, he was sure. And, looking up, he noticed gloomily that the wallpaper was starting to curl away at the top of the walls, no doubt loosened by damp and mildew.

No, everything was just as depressing as it had been last term and the term before – except that now things looked even more worn and seedy.

But his thoughts had been interrupted on the landing by sudden darkness. He sighed. No doubt the lights had fused in the storm. If that wasn't just the last straw! With a groan he took off his dripping coat and laid it over the banisters; then he felt his way to the cupboard at the bottom of the stairs which housed the fuse-box. He opened the door and peered into the blackness. Struggling to find the box of matches and the candle left in the cupboard to deal with such emergencies, Mr Fox finally got a flame going and looked around for the fuse-box.

And that was when he heard a faint giggling sound.

"Who's there!" he barked. "It's way past everyone's bedtime. Come on – show yourself!"

The giggling continued – and Mr Fox, emboldened by the few drinks he'd had that evening, leant even further into the cupboard, stretching the candle as far as he could to see into its dark recesses. He could make out nothing but a collection of dusty old school photographs from 1910, bags of broken chalk, curling old timetables, battered mortar boards and yellowing files. He also noticed a half-full bottle of whisky which he'd dumped quickly a couple of years ago when he thought he'd heard someone coming along the corridor. He grabbed it and put it under his jacket.

But that was beside the point. Yes, there was certainly someone in there. He could hear breathing – broken by the occasional high-pitched giggle.

"Out! Out!" ordered Mr Fox furiously – and from behind a huge pile of old exam papers marked Matriculation (so that was where they'd got to!) stepped the weirdest creature Mr Fox had ever seen.

It was boy-sized, but its head was rather too big for its body. It was covered with very thin, wispy hair and had extra-large unblinking eyes. Its chest seemed much too big, its legs were very short and thin, and the creature was covered in thick clothes from top to bottom. This wouldn't have been surprising except for the fact that it was summer – and you don't expect to see boys in heavy woollen socks, shirts buttoned right up to the neck and big woolly gloves when it's hot. As a final touch, the creature's skin definitely had a kind of greenish tinge to it.

As this peculiar person stepped daintily out of the cupboard and extended his gloved hand, Mr Fox automatically responded, rubbing his head in astonishment. Then the creature, in a very peculiar piping voice, said, "Good evening, sire."

How many drinks had Mr Fox had at the Stoat and Otter, he wondered? Surely not *that* many! He was half tempted to return the bottle of whisky to the dusty shelf but thought better of it.

"Sire? I am 'sir' not 'sire'!" said Mr Fox, recovering his poise and holding the candle nearer the strange boy's face. "What on earth were you doing in my cupboard! Whose class are you in? I shall have you reported to the headmaster! I mean, I shall report you to the headmaster myself. Myself being the headmaster. I shall report you to myself!"

The creature took a long deep breath and as he did so Mr Fox noticed the flame on his candle guttered perilously.

"Prithee forgive me, for being ensconced in yon cupboard," replied the creature. "I was betaking myself of some sleep."

"Sleep? You should sleep in your dormitory, unless you have a study!" cried Mr Fox. "Whose class are you in? And how old are you?"

"'Tis only now that I have hastened to this seat of learning," replied the creature. "I wouldst have come before but I have been travelling with my mother and father on a universal cruise and thus have been delayed."

"Universal cruise?" Mr Fox rubbed his forehead. "What are you talking about? Do you mean 'world' cruise?"

"Indeed I do, prithee," said the creature. "As for my age I am one score years less a decade."

"If you're ten, why can't you say so!" said Mr Fox. "That means you're in a dormitory. But what did you say about this world cruise?" Anyone, reasoned Mr Fox rapidly, whose parents could afford to take their son on a world cruise must surely be absolutely rolling in money – enough to contribute generously to the new science block.

"We traversed the stars each, the Northern Lights, the meteors and variously in space."

"You what?" said Mr Fox, but more benignly now, his mind on the generous donation he was set on squeezing from this strange boy's parents. "Perhaps you mean that you went to the – er – Far East, saw the – ah – Northern Lights – oh, went to Blackpool, eh? – and Mexico and perhaps, er, the Greek island of Spetsai?"

The creature looked a bit confused, which Mr Fox took to be a sign of agreement.

"And might I ask why you are wearing gloves? Your style of dress is hardly suitable for life at Burlap Hall, you know," said Mr Fox, eyeing the stranger up and down. Now he got a better look at the boy – if, indeed, it was a boy – there was no doubt that he was, well, not like other boys, although he couldn't put his finger on what exactly was wrong. His face was pale, flat and expressionless except for his darting, watery eyes. Mr

Fox felt his flesh crawl slightly at the sight of him.

"'Tis eczema, sire," replied the creature, looking rather sad. "Enshrouded must my hands be, lest my skin dry and withered becomes."

"Hmm. Well, we don't want your skin getting withered, do we?" said Mr Fox, uneasily. He stepped back a few paces. He hoped it wasn't catching. "Now tell me what your name is. I can't recall getting a form of registration from your parents, I must say. But no matter. No doubt it is somewhere in my correspondence. You'll be in Mrs Grain's class. But I'll need your parents' address so I can write to them confirming your arrival. And, of course, to ask if they would contribute to the new science block."

"Zounds! A science block! By Jupiter!" piped the creature. "My name is Orcon and my address is far away. Far away. I will send word to my mother and father and inform them in my missive of the science block."

"You will?" Mr Fox cheered up. "I'll show you the drawings tomorrow so you can describe what we're planning. I hope your parents will be collecting you at the end of term and then I can ask them myself. I don't think I've yet had the pleasure ..."

Mr Fox tried to remember meeting the boy's parents, but his mind was a blank. It was that final whisky. He shouldn't have had it.

"Indeed, most surely, prithee, sire," said Orcon. "Now lead me, if you will, to my sleeping quarters." He picked up a small, glittering holdall in his gloved hand.

"Hold on, hold on," snapped Mr Fox. He was slightly taken aback by this command – and there was the fuse-box to fix. "I've got to get the lights working first."

"Prithee, allow me," said the strange creature, stepping daintily back into the cupboard. He stared at the fuse-box briefly and then passed a gloved hand over it. Immediately all the lights sprang back to life. Mr Fox was so surprised that the candle dropped from his hand. Orcon bent to pick it up, extinguished it, placed it back in the cupboard and shut the door.

"And now – my dormitory," he said, with a sweeping gesture to show he expected to be led there at once.

Mr Fox simply blinked. He really *must* have drunk far too much. Trying to get a grip on himself, he led the way to a dormitory, and arranged for a bed to be made up.

"Well, goodnight, er, Orcon," he said, wondering, as he said it, what kind of weird name that was. "Sweet dreams. And welcome to Burlap Hall."

"Hist, wist, prithee and perchance," replied Orcon, a peculiar smile spreading over his greenish face. "My humble thanks to thee, kind sire." He then scrambled into bed, fully clothed.

Mr Fox felt too tired to remonstrate with him, particularly when the other children in the dormitory started getting out of bed and peering at the new arrival, giggling at his big head and his wispy hair. "Back to bed! All of you!" he snapped. He switched off the light and left to get some sleep himself.

When he woke the following day and remembered the events of the night before, he felt a strange surge of excitement inside himself. Couldst Orcon be the goose that laid the golden egg? Prithee, hist and wist, perchance he'd stumbled on a source of guineas that had nary slip'd his way before?

Dammit, he thought, as a sharp headache stealthily

25

crept over his left eye. His hangover was even making him *think* in Orcon's ridiculous language. He'd have to sort out the new boy's way of talking as soon as possible. He sounded like a half-wit from the sixteenth century. He just hoped Orcon's parents didn't talk the same way. Or, worse still, view money in the same way. Because in the sixteenth century a hundred pounds was a kind of fortune that could last a family for years and buy a stately home into the bargain. But these days a hundred pounds would be just a drop in the ocean.

Sighing, he slipped from his bed and, removing his pair of fraying blue and white striped pyjamas, began to dress.

When Tom got back to his room, Miles had been joined by Susan who was already dressed and was busy copying out Tom's homework herself.

"Wow, you must be clever to do this!" she said. "I couldn't work this out in a million years."

"You know why that is, don't you?" said Miles, winking at Tom.

"It's *not* because I'm a girl," said Susan, flushing furiously. "Honestly, you guys, you're so sexist ..."

"Who said anything about being a girl?" said Miles. "No, I'll tell you why. It's because your brain is *extremely* small."

"I thought all girls' brains were bigger than boys' because they were covered with an extra layer of fat," said Tom mischievously.

"Making them thicker," added Miles.

Susan turned furiously.

"And cleverer," said Tom, tactfully. "Did you know that dinosaurs' brains were absolutely minute? Their brains were so small and their bodies were so big that if you pinched them on the tail it took half an hour before they said 'Ouch'."

"Dinosaurs did not say 'Ouch'!" said Susan, scribbling away. "They said 'OOOUURGH!'"

Tom stared thoughtfully at his scuffed shoes, wondered if they needed a polish, decided they did and then decided to do nothing about them. He then started to get dressed. He rather wished Susan wouldn't drop into their room quite so early. True, she was their best friend and did have a room over the corridor, but he always felt embarrassed getting dressed when she was around. He had to pull on his pants and trousers really quickly while she wasn't looking – and he didn't like her looking at his chest because every time she saw it Tom felt she was counting the number of hairs on it. As there were none, it only made things worse.

There was no such problem today, however. Both Miles and Susan were so engrossed in copying out the pages of computer prep that they didn't look up from their work.

He made one last attempt to tell them about the night before.

"You won't believe it when I tell you how I managed to do that homework last night," he started. "There was this clap of thunder and then suddenly the computer started sending messages to me asking if it could hel—"

"Shh!" said Miles, frowning with concentration as he copied furiously. "What does this mean? 590 LPRINT CHR$(27) + CHR$(10) ...?"

It was no good. They wouldn't listen.

CHAPTER THREE

Mr Fox sat down at his desk feeling completely scrambled. First there was this weird new boy, then Mr Carstairs had told him that all the computers had gone wrong due to the electricity fusing the night before, then there were the builders.

He'd just returned from consulting them and as a result he feared he'd made an enormous mistake in hiring them. Admittedly they were the cheapest builders that Mr Fox could find, but when he discovered that none of them knew what a laboratory was and kept calling it a lavatory and asking him why he wanted one so big when they could fix him up a nice small one with a neat flushing system, much cheaper, he did rather question their competence.

On his desk were all kinds of other problems – like a message from Miss Shepherd, the cookery and crafts teacher, asking if she could see him for a moment. He knew what that meant – a couple of hours as she wittered on about astral planes and psychic phenomena before she screwed up enough courage to get to the point, most likely only a request for more string for her macramé classes.

There was also a note from Signor Ruzzi demanding the return of the piano tuner. The music teacher had been practising for his special twice-termly Leisure Music performance and had found the F-sharp too sharp. Mr Fox winced. *He* wouldn't like to play on keys that were too sharp; they must cut your fingers dreadfully.

And just as he was about to get down to making a

list of the sports day events – after writing to St Beowulf's to complain about their umpiring of the cricket match last weekend (it was surely impossible that Burlap Hall could have been bowled out for four runs) – there was a knock on the door. Mr Fox sighed.

"Come in," he said, wearily putting down his pen.

It was Mr Carstairs.

"Great news!" he said, pulling up a chair and sitting in it enthusiastically. It might be difficult to imagine someone sitting in a chair enthusiastically, but Mr Carstairs did everything enthusiastically. Before he sat in the chair he looked eager and excited at the prospect of sitting down and, once seated, he leant forward as if he just couldn't wait to experience the enormous fun of getting up again. His eyes were bright, his cheeks pink with the exertion of having just completed a three-mile jog (he took games as well) and he rubbed his hands in a thrilled kind of way as if he'd just discovered an oil well under the squash courts.

Mr Carstairs was one of those people known in schools as an "all-rounder". As a boy his only disappointment had been to find that there was no university course in all-rounding, but had there been he would have received a double first. He was English teacher, Games Master, general organizer and now Computer Studies teacher as well.

"Great news!" repeated Mr Carstairs. "I've sorted out the electrical problems and I've finally got rid of the bugs from the Apples. And, best of all, the virus that had attacked them doesn't appear to have spread."

Mr Fox was horrified. "Bugs! Viruses! Good God, Carstairs, we must get hold of the medical supervisor as soon as possible!" A plague of bugs was just what Nutter would leap on as an excuse to close down the school. "We can't have this school being a breeding ground for disease! Isn't there a vaccine we can get hold of? And if they're in the apples, we must get rid of them forthwith. Throw them away!"

"Throw the Apples away?" Mr Carstairs looked horrified. "But Headmaster, we've just spent thousands of pounds on them!"

"Thousands of pounds on apples?" Mr Fox leapt in his seat. "We haven't got thousands of pounds to spare! You must be mad!"

"But we can keep them and use them – there's nothing wrong with them!" protested Mr Carstairs.

"Nothing wrong with them! They'll be full of holes! They'll be rotten!"

A look of relief came over Mr Carstairs' face as he understood.

"No, no, no," he said. "I'm talking of Apples. With a capital A."

"Capital A or not, they'll still be rotten. Lemons are sour whether they're spelt with a capital or a small l," riposted Mr Fox furiously.

"No, no … Apples," said Mr Carstairs. "Computers. You know, full of kilobytes." Seeing Mr Fox's confused face, he repeated slowly, "Kilo … bytes."

"Kilos of apples? For thousands of pounds? With bites in them as well as bugs? Surely you could have got them cheaper!"

"No, no," said Mr Carstairs, clutching his forehead in frustration. "Our computers are Apples. Viruses are problems that can affect them and bugs are mistakes in programs."

Mr Fox groaned inwardly. That was the trouble with Computer Studies. He simply couldn't make head or tail of them. And here was Mr Carstairs saying that he was using apples for computers. No doubt it all made sense in the mysterious world of pixcels, files, kilobytes and ASCII files that Mr Carstairs inhabited, but it was all Greek to Mr Fox. Although even Greek seemed easier to understand than Computerese.

"Well, I'm delighted," he said, in an unsure voice that did not belie his ignorance. "No viruses, you say. Excellent. And no, er, cockroaches or, er, wriggly things. Well done."

Mr Carstairs cheered up. "Headmaster, you must let me try to explain computers to you. They're a fascinating subject. They are the culture of the future. Forget Darwin, forget Shakespeare, forget Pythagoras. Computers are where our future lies. And this course we've just embarked on is a great step for Burlap Hall, a step into the twentieth century. It's really – er – def." (Mr Carstairs had just watched a television programme aimed at "Youth Today" and learned that the word "def" was the latest thing, meaning brilliant, super or generally splendid.)

"What?" said Mr Fox, irritably. The damned chap was using computer language again.

"Def," said Mr Carstairs. "It means …"

"Just because I say 'what' doesn't mean I'm deaf," snapped Mr Fox. "I can hear perfectly well. Now is there anything else you have to tell me? I'm extremely busy at the moment."

Mr Carstairs gave a sigh and got up. It was no use. The headmaster was a nice enough old stick, but Mr Fox would never understand the language of the "now" generation. He was definitely of the "then" generation. Well, at least he had tried. Mr Carstairs left; he had a class to take.

*   *   *

"I couldn't do the homework, sir," said Sheila as Mr Carstairs sprang into the classroom. All the pupils lounged at their desks looking bored.

Mr Carstairs sat down and turned over the pages of his vast computer book. He became so fascinated that it was only the sound of Simon coughing that reminded him he should be teaching.

"I couldn't do it either!" said Rosemary.

There was a general chorus of agreement from most of the class.

Tom was about to signal to Susan and Miles that it might be best not to hand in the homework, particularly as no one else could do it and he didn't understand it himself, when Susan smugly put up her hand. "I could do it, sir," she said. "And so could Miles and Tom."

"Well, let's see how far you got," said Mr Carstairs, getting up and collecting the work.

Tom groaned inwardly.

"Well done!" said Mr Carstairs, as he put the papers down on his desk. "Perhaps you should have tried harder, Sheila. Or you could always have asked me last night. But I can't understand how none of you could manage it, quite honestly. All I was asking you was – where was the question?" He looked down at his *Computers for Beginners* book. "Yes, here we are, page 14, question nine: 'Describe what a pixcel is in your own words. Use diagrams if you wish.'"

"Pixcels!" snorted Asquith Minor. "Everyone knows what a pixcel is!"

"I don't," muttered a small spotty boy in the front.

"I thought they were things you found at the bottom of your garden, with fairies and elves," giggled a new girl.

"But you asked us to do question nine on page 40,

not 14!" protested Simon.

"Yes – you did, sir," chorused the others. "We couldn't do it!"

Mr Carstairs leafed over the pages and found it. "'Explain the generation of the bit image, using examples'," he murmured. "But we haven't done bits! No wonder you couldn't do it."

"You see!" said Asquith Minor triumphantly. "It was impossible."

"I'm sorry," said Mr Carstairs. "My mistake. Now let's turn to where we left off yesterday and continue with – but hang on," he added. He drummed his pencil suspiciously on the desk. "How come you three other kids managed to do this homework?" He picked up Tom's papers and studied them closely. The work was so complicated he could hardly understand it himself. "This is very advanced stuff," he said, fixing Tom with a scowl. "It's not possible you did this on your own, surely?"

"I did," replied Tom, truthfully. Well, nearly truthfully. He'd pressed all the keys, after all.

Mr Carstairs picked up the other papers handed in by Miles and Susan. "I don't see how you could have managed this – and they're all the same," he added, leafing through them. "What's going on?"

There was a silence – the horrible silence that hangs over a class when someone has done something wrong and the teacher waits for a confession. Then a sneaky, high-pitched voice piped up at the back.

"Sire, 'twas I who did it! 'Twas not they!"

Mr Carstairs looked confused. "'Twas thee?" he said. Then he corrected himself. "I mean – it was you? You mean they copied it from you? Then where's your homework, might I ask? And who are you, anyway? I don't recognize you."

"Prithee, sire, I am late arrived last night. Late because my parents were on a universal – I mean world – cruise. These lusty youths didst ask my aid and thus I did provide assistance from my store of knowledge."

"You mean you told them the answers?"

"Yes, sire."

Tom was about to turn and see who on earth was speaking, but Mr Carstairs checked him. "Look at me, Buxton!" he snapped. "What have you got to say for yourself, eh? I'm ashamed of you all! Letting yourselves down like this! Letting all of us down!"

Miles sighed quietly to himself. Hey ho, here it came, the usual rubbish.

"Letting your parents down, letting the school down – by cheating! You three will all miss the special Leisure Music performance before supper today, and stay in for a detention. I'm ashamed of you! Letting yourselves down, letting the school down ..." On and on he droned, like a broken record.

Resigned to his punishment, Tom turned to look at the new face at the back of the class, but it was hidden behind other pupils and couldn't be seen.

"As for you – er ..."

"Orcon," piped the voice.

"Orcon. Obviously you have a vast knowledge of computers. I hope you'll be a keen participant in our studies. But another time – never help people with their homework. OK?"

"Aye, sire," replied Orcon, apparently oblivious of the fact that everyone else in the class was splitting their sides every time he opened his mouth. Asquith Minor was mouthing, "Sire, prithee" to the world in general and pretending to be a cavalier making a bow at his desk.

Miles whispered to Tom, "Who's that little git? Is it true what he said?"

Tom just shrugged. He couldn't understand what was going on. He tried to speak but was quelled by another furious look from Mr Carstairs.

It was by no means the end of the world to miss Leisure Music with Signor Ruzzi. There were two such periods during each term, for which Signor Ruzzi practised assiduously. He would take a composer – like Chopin or Mozart – and give a short talk on his life, illustrated with musical examples.

This time Ruzzi had picked the Russian composer, Alexander Scriabin, not a musician very easy on the ear, but just up Signor Ruzzi's street, being sufficiently mystical and weird to satisfy his peculiar taste.

Everyone in the school was forced to sit and listen to the lecture; most of the pupils brought Tintin books which they read concealed in copies of the music that Signor Ruzzi encouraged them to follow while he played.

Orcon sat between Asquith Minor and Sheila, both of whom felt most ill-at-ease with their new class-mate.

"Ist special language, pray?" asked Orcon of Asquith Minor, staring puzzledly at the notes on the score.

"Don't you know what that is?" said Asquith Minor, derisively. "It's notes. Music. You know."

The children in the row in front giggled uncontrollably when they overheard Orcon's question. One of them, dared by his friends, turned round and suddenly said, "You've got a big head, big-head!" and then turned back, creased up with laughter.

Emboldened by his friend's success, another boy

looked round, "Your hair's funny!" he tittered. "And your eyes are too big!" Then he turned back again.

Signor Ruzzi was droning on about Skriabin and how the Russian tried to convey mystical and philosphical theories in large orchestral works, while Asquith Minor dolefully scribbled on his score. "Skriabin," he said. "Screwy. Should have been put in a bin."

The children in front started tittering again. "Like your friend!" said one, turning round, mischievously. "What's wrong with his fingers, eh? It's rude to wear gloves indoors."

"Silenzio!" roared Signor Ruzzi, overhearing the chattering. His huge moustache trembled at the ends. "Is no good these bad manners for our learned Russian composer. Show more aspect!"

"Respect, you mean!" said a cheeky boy from the back.

"Respect for the Russian!" intoned Signor Ruzzi. He turned to the piano, sat down and played a chord. "And now – some examples of his great works."

He lifted his hands high, then crashed his fingers onto the keys. Off he went, twiddly bits here, twiddly bits there, arpeggios, quiet bits, loud bits, weird bits and crashing chords. The great hall resounded with the notes. Asquith Minor looked up wearily at the bits of stained glass left in the windows. Most of it had been damaged in the war but there were still some pictures left and in the fading sunlight he was sure he could see the figures moving, stuffing their fingers in their ears. Every time the children thought the performance was over and started to clap, Signor Ruzzi would put a finger to his lips and then continue with yet another movement.

Orcon was listening intently, his pointed ears pricked

for every sound. Sheila, finding his presence disconcerting, moved her chair slightly away.

The children in front turned round and started laughing again. "Can't bear to sit next to him?" said one, putting his finger to his head and turning it around, implying Orcon was barmy. "Don't blame you. He's weird!"

But at this Asquith Minor, who was not a cruel boy, whispered, "Oh, shut up! Stop it!"

"Oh, is he your friend?"

"Just shut up!"

"Who said you were a monitor!" "Sorry, *sir*!"

Gradually their voices got louder and louder teasing and arguing until Signor Ruzzi came to the end of his piece. There was desultory clapping. Everyone's bottoms ached with sitting on the uncomfortable chairs and, as they were all starving and longing to get their supper, they hoped Signor Ruzzi would wind up his talk quickly. Unfortunately the music teacher held up a hand. His face was suffused with anger.

"Why clap?" he asked, sarcastically. "I wonder any of you could hear any of this work so brilliant, with the noise going on from that corner. Yes!" he said, pinning a furious look on Asquith Minor. "I mean you! You and your friends!"

Asquith Minor went bright red as the entire school turned round to stare at him.

"Perhaps you would like to come up and play some Skriabin for us!" he snapped. "It takes years and years of practice to perfect a piece like this – but no doubt you can play it perfectly. Perhaps you would care to demonstrate your musical skills to us! Come up here and try! Never have I so insulted been …!"

Asquith Minor was rooted to his chair. He didn't

know where to look. He wanted to sink through the floor. Other pupils in the school were muttering rude remarks at him and laughing. Then Orcon put up his gloved hand.

"Prithee, kind music teacher," he said. "Allow me to play the piece instead of my friend here." And without further ado, he rose from his chair, pushed past the other children in his row and walked to the piano.

Signor Ruzzi was struck dumb at the sight of this strange creature. Orcon's big head wobbled slightly on his thin neck and his skin radiated a greenish glow.

"Who are you?" asked the music teacher. "You with gloves. In those gloves you cannot play!"

Orcon simply gave him a piercing stare and sat down at the piano. He looked at the keys and then at the music. Then he reached up, folded up the music and put it on the floor. "Distracting," he murmured. Then he started.

His gloved hands flew across the keys so fast they became a blur. He played perfectly – an incredible display from beginning to end, but at about ten times the speed of Signor Ruzzi, who stood by dumbfounded.

When Orcon had finished, to a great roar of cheers and boos, the music master came over to him. "Extraordinary!" he said, shaking his head. "Never have I heard anything so extraordinary …" But at that moment the bell rang for supper and there was a great scraping of chairs as everyone got up and hurried to the dining room as quickly as possible.

Tom, Miles and Susan also heard the bell and, glad to finish their detentions, walked eagerly to the dining room. They squeezed on to the long school benches, getting splinters in the backs of their legs in the process. Tom stared gloomily at the lines of old food and fat that were lodged in the woodgrain of the table-top. He didn't feel at all hungry. He hated detentions. Particularly when they were unfair. He glanced resentfully down the other end of the table where Mr Carstairs was helping Mr Fox to potatoes. And anyway, what did this new boy mean when he said he'd done Tom's homework for him? He hadn't. Tom had never met him.

Asquith Minor and Simon were sitting nearby, giggling about Signor Ruzzi's performance and imitating the voice of the curious new pupil, when Orcon himself appeared and slipped in beside them. He smiled at Asquith Minor. Since he had defended him against the teasing of the other pupils, he saw him as a friend.

"Prithee, may I take leave to join you?" asked the funny little creature – and sat down without further ado.

"No!" hissed Miles, furiously, leaning over Tom to glare at the strange newcomer. "Tell-tale!"

Orcon was about to reply when he was interrupted by Simon's laughter.

"Prithee …!" he chortled, pointing at Orcon. "What kind of language is that, for heaven's sake?"

"Why laughest thou?" asked Orcon. His big pale face showed blank puzzlement and his eyes watered more than usual.

"Because of the way you talk!" chortled Sheila through gales of giggles.

"What ails my speech?" asked Orcon, confused.

"It's like something from the fifteenth century – or the sixteenth or seventeenth, I don't know," said Miles, grinning from ear to ear.

"Gadzooks!" said Orcon. He looked extremely worried. Simon was repeating "Gadzooks!" to himself until he could hardly breathe for laughing so much.

Orcon slipped a woollen glove into his shirt and twiddled about inside. He was feeling for a point just above his belt on his left-hand side.

"What-ho!" he burst out, suddenly. "What a jolly spiffing lark, eh what? A jolly jape and spanking wheeze don'tcha know! Don't snitch on me, you chaps, will you? What a whizzo place this is, chums!"

Miles and Tom gawped at him.

"Now you're talking like a schoolboy from the 1920s!" said Miles.

"Oo-er ... Crumbs! What a bogging bish!" exclaimed Orcon, reaching once more inside his shirt. "Hey, man, how about this? This cool enough for you cats? What a drag about the speech patterns. You must have thought I was a real square instead of a swinging hep-cat like you guys."

Despite himself, Asquith Minor was laughing so much he had got out his handkerchief. Even the arrival of one of the boot-faced serving ladies coming round with large plates of beef, carrots and potatoes couldn't stop him. The lady plonked a plate crossly in front of each pupil.

By this time Simon was hysterical. They were all making such a noise that boys and girls around them stopped talking and stared.

Finally Miles calmed himself down enough to say, "How do you do it? You seem to be able to change from century to century – and now you're talking like people in the sixties. We're getting to the end of the twentieth century, you know."

Orcon looked relieved at the news. "Right on, man,"

he said, reaching inside his shirt and twiddling again. This time he craned his huge head between the buttons and appeared to be looking at something. "Sorry to be so uncool." Finally he seemed to have got what he wanted and started to speak – but no sound came out of his mouth. He looked furious. He banged himself angrily on the chest a few times and then started coughing.

"OK, I think I've got it right now. Sorry about that," he said. "I should be OK now, all right?"

Tom nodded in amazement.

"Now I must get on with my supper," said Orcon. He stared at his plate and then at everyone else around him, none of whom had started to eat, so mesmerised were they by his extraordinary performance.

He looked uncertain. He picked up a potato with a gloved hand and shook it over his plate as if it were a pepperpot. He then took a metal pepperpot from the table and placed it in the middle of his dish. And finally he picked up two of the longest carrots from his plate and, using them like a knife and fork, proceeded to pick up the pepperpot and cram it into his mouth, chewing the metal happily as he did so.

"Delicious," he said, between munches. And then, noticing everyone staring at him, he gave his peculiar smile. He had that rather shy, idiotic look on his face that people have when they're feeling absolutely terrible inside but are pretending that everything's fine on the surface. And everyone knew he'd realized he'd done something wrong because he suddenly started giggling.

And that was when everything fell into place for Tom. Goose-pimples erupted on his skin, a rash of sweat sprang on to his forehead and, as the truth dawned, his heart thumped with fear.

Yes, Orcon had been telling the truth when he claimed to have done Tom's homework for him. Because that giggle was exactly the same giggle he'd heard the night before in the computer room!

CHAPTER FOUR

The quiet giggling continued until it was drowned by the sound of other kids all laughing and pointing.

"He's eating the pepperpot with a pair of carrots!" one small boy tittered, hiding his mouth with his hand.

"He's got his carrot the wrong way up," giggled another.

And as Orcon started to put some peas into his mouth, another commented, "You shouldn't eat peas off your carrot!"

Rosemary warned, "Watch out! Your carrot might be too sharp!"

This went on until Orcon slowly stopped giggling. He put down his carrots and stared at his plate. He then carefully watched someone eating further down the table, took the mangled pepperpot from his mouth and put it back on the table, picked up his knife and fork and started eating normally.

But it was too late. Children were already getting up from other tables to see what was up; suppressed giggles were erupting at Orcon's end of the table until, suddenly, he snapped.

He looked up from his plate, his large face contorted with rage. His wispy hair rose dangerously on his head and started waving around. Then he pointed, with a gloved finger, at a small, giggling boy. His victim was Arthur Mitsford, a sad, undergrown little chap who was inclined to burst into fits of laughter or floods of tears at the slightest provocation.

"You!" he said, peremptorily. "How old are you?"

"I'm ni-hi-hi-ha-ha-ne!" giggled Arthur.

"Right. You're younger than me. That means I can make you do exactly what I like!"

"No you can't!" said Susan, leaning over the table. "You bully!"

Orcon didn't hear. He leant over and fixed Arthur with a terrible gaze. His eyes seemed to grow bigger and brighter until out of them, burning like laser beams, glowed two fearsome green rays.

"Pick up that glass of water!" he commanded, wagging his woolly finger at Arthur who was now silent, transfixed by Orcon's gaze like a rabbit caught in the headlights of a car. Trembling, Arthur did so. "Now, pour it over Mr Fox!" said Orcon in a high-pitched whisper. "That'll teach you to laugh at me!"

Little Arthur didn't hesitate. Solemnly, he climbed from the bench and, picking up the glass of water, walked slowly towards Mr Fox. He walked past the pile of trays where you collected your knives and forks; past the water fountain and past the set of steaming metal boxes where you could go up and ask for second helpings – not that anyone ever did, of course. He passed the lower forms' tables, then the middle school, then the older children. The whole dining room fell into a complete hush. Some children put out their hands and tried to prevent the boy from being so foolish, but he walked on, hypnotized.

Finally he reached the teachers' end of the table and Mr Fox, who was trying with little success to persuade Mrs Grain, the Latin teacher, to supervise the long-jump event at the school's sports day. "I will do anything I can to help," she was saying. "I will make the tea, I will organize the prizes, I will even clear up afterwards – but I'm afraid supervising the long-jump is beyond me. My strengths are intellectual, as you must know."

Mr Fox was relieved to spot Arthur Mitsford coming up to him. He despaired of organizing sports day. It would be a fiasco as usual. He looked up as the child approached. "Yes, you may be excused," he said, automatically.

Arthur said nothing. His eyes looked dead and dull. He extended the hand with the glass of water in it, solemnly moved it over Mr Fox's head and poured the water straight over the headmaster's bald pate.

The water ran down Mr Fox's face, down the sides of his nose and neck, soaking his collar; the long strand of hair, that he trailed unsuccessfully to cover his balding head, came astray and hung down one side like a piece of wet string. His eyebrows lost their bristle and clung limply to his skin like shipwrecked sailors to a rock. For a moment he was stunned; then his eyes bulged furiously as if one of his famous looks was about to erupt – and finally, eyebrows recovering their bounce, nostrils flaring and the water on his face turning to steam, he turned the full vent of his rage on little Arthur. He pushed back his chair and rose up, towering above the small boy.

"What is the meaning of this!" he yelled furiously, shaking himself. "This is *preposterous* behaviour! I will not stand for it!"

Mr Fox's fury broke Arthur's trance and the child was visibly shaken, staring first at Mr Fox, then at the glass in his hand, then at Mr Fox again. Then he burst into tears.

"You should be ashamed of yourself!" declared Mr Fox. "You've let the school down, you've let yourself down …" ("Here we go again," whispered Miles to Tom.) "You've let your parents down, you've let your

45

class down, you've let the whole ..."

Arthur stood and howled as the entire school stared in horrified fascination. Only Asquith Minor, Tom noticed, was gazing at Orcon with a certain astonished respect.

"You will do four detentions a day for a week!" declared Mr Fox. "And come and see me in my study!"

He turned on his heel and departed for the cloakroom. He had never felt so humiliated in his life. He stood alone among the lockers and rows of hanging coats and shook himself like a dog. Then he stared at himself in the mirror. Soaked! His whole head and the top of his shirt was completely soaked! What was the world coming to? He wouldn't be surprised if the children started mugging the teachers in the corridors. Who knew, he might himself be mugged! As he rubbed vigorously at his one strand of hair with a towel and combed it carefully back over his dome, the thought grew in his mind. After all, he'd read enough about violence in schools, about pupils attacking their teachers with iron bars. This could be the tip of the iceberg.

It was small wonder, with these thoughts going through his head, that when Miss Shepherd accosted him as he emerged from the cloakroom he gave a yelp of fear. He cowered visibly before recovering himself. After all, if anyone was going to mug him it was hardly likely to be the thin, red-nosed crafts and cookery teacher.

"Are you all right?" she twittered, twisting her hands. "What a terrible experience. But do you really think that four detentions a day for a whole week is the right approach? Perhaps it's his nerves? Should we call a doctor? It's so unlike little Arthur. He's such a sweet, gentle soul."

"Sweet! Gentle! My dear Miss Shepherd, you can hardly call him that," said Mr Fox. "He's a thug in the making! Today a glass of water, tomorrow a lager lout!" And yet he, too, was surprised that of all children it should be Arthur who had behaved so badly. Arthur was continually in tears or giggles and his one pleasure was to grow seeds in a little box on the sill of the window by his bed – sometimes singing to them to encourage them to sprout.

He was about to reply when Mr Roy, the geography teacher, came hurrying towards them, wiping his mouth with a paper napkin in case a stray lentil had attached itself to his upper lip.

"Red meat!" he said, emphatically. "That's what it is. Red meat."

A small boy rushed by giggling, prompting Mr Fox to open the door to the gym and usher the two teachers inside. "More privacy," he explained. He sat down on a vaulting horse and looked up at Mr Roy. "You were saying?"

"Red meat," repeated Mr Roy, "promotes violence. Put him on a vegetarian, sugar-free diet and he'll be mild as mustard in no time."

"Mild as mustard?" asked Miss Shepherd. "Surely …"

"Mild as … a melon," said Mr Roy. "Quite honestly, Mr Fox, if this isn't proof enough that we should all be on a vegetarian diet, I don't know what is. Not only do reports prove but statistics also show …" he pulled a much-thumbed piece of paper from the Vegetarian Society from his back pocket, "that …"

"Yes, yes, yes, yes, another time." Mr Fox was getting fed up with all this attention. Funny, he thought, how upset you could get over something when everyone was trying to tell you it was nothing; but the moment people rushed round and stared at you with shocked faces it didn't seem so important. And after all, it was only water. "I'll have a chat with the boy. Maybe something's bothering him. Forget it. A one-off. The less attention we draw to it the better. This is not the moment to focus too much on disruptive behaviour. Who knows, there might be a spurt of it if we don't watch out. And that's the last thing we want, with Clive Nutter coming to inspect the school. Or have I not mentioned this to you? Yes," he added, noticing their horrified faces, "Clive Nutter himself."

"Clive Nutter!" said Mr Roy. "That little creep! You'd better not let me near him, or there'll be trouble. We used to teach at the same school fifteen years ago. He deserves to be strung up and shot!" He picked up a weight and waved it aggressively.

"This is unlike you, Mr Roy, I must say," said Mr Fox, unable to resist a smile. "Are you sure you haven't been indulging in red meat yourself recently?"

At the sight of Mr Roy's shocked face, he got up and clapped him on the shoulder. Mr Roy dropped the weight on his foot and tried not to scream. "Just my little joke," said the headmaster. "You're absolutely right about Nutter. But there's nothing we can do about it, I'm afraid."

"Shouldn't we hold a teachers' meeting?" said Miss Shepherd. "I think we ought to plan a strategy to deal with him, don't you? You remember what happened about the medical supplies – and the kitchens … It has to be said that although I wish no harm to anyone, even I find myself making a little exception when it comes to Mr Nutter."

"A meeting. Good idea," said Mr Fox. "And then we can discuss sports day as well. I was hoping, Miss

Shepherd, that since I know you have had experience of ballet dancing – which, of course, involves long leaps – you would help us out by supervising the long-jump. I can think of no one more suitable."

Miss Shepherd went pink with pleasure. "Of course, Headmaster!" she said, flattered.

Cheered by the support he was getting from his staff he added, "Come, let us finish our meal." And, as a group of boys and girls in shorts burst into the gym and started springing on the trampoline and clambering up bars, he offered his arm to Miss Shepherd and accompanied her back to the dining room.

It wasn't until the Latin lesson with Mrs Grain that Tom had a chance to explain his suspicions to Miles. Mrs Grain wanted every pupil in the class to translate into Latin some deadly piece of prose about Caesar's army and everyone had to take turns.

"What's the point of translating it back into Latin if it's already been translated into English?" grumbled Miles, as he stared at the piece, his mind boggling.

"Oh, I don't know," whispered Tom, impatiently. "But Miles, listen. I think Orcon *did* do my computer prep! He's telling the truth!"

"He didn't arrive till the day after, stupid!" said Miles. "How could he have done it?"

"*Erat demonstrandum,*" said Mrs Grain, patting her tidy bun. "When the nominative is in the accusative, the subjective always takes the subjunctive, *except* when using the pluperfect imperfect." (Or at least that's what it sounded like to Tom.)

"I was doing my prep when there was this clap of thunder and I slammed all the keys down and suddenly the computer started telling me how to do my homework," whispered Tom. "Then after that it told me I had to press some buttons and there was another flash of lightning and out he popped."

"Out who popped?" whispered Susan, who was on Tom's left, listening avidly.

"Orcon, of course."

"But how do you mean, 'out he popped'? Did he climb through the screen?"

"I don't know. It was too dark. I couldn't see anything, but I'm certain it was him. He pushed by me in the dark and he had that dreadful giggle," said Tom, worriedly.

"Maybe he's from ..." said Susan, but was stopped by Mrs Grain glaring at her.

"Susan, are you paying attention?" she snapped. "Orcon is just about to translate 'Caesar's cohorts sent many arrows into the phalanx over the hill. Having been defeated, the general deployed his troops into the woods. Having experienced three continuous reverses ...'"

("What's a cohort?" whispered Miles to Tom. "Probably the singular of phalanx," said Tom. "Or maybe it's a deployed phalanx, whatever deployed means. Why did Caesar spend his time deploying his cohorts, anyway? Did he do nothing else with his life? A tragic waste, I say, of a great man.")

But after a high-pitched cough and, Tom noticed, more twiddling with whatever he'd been twiddling with under his shirt before, Orcon started to translate: *"Praeterea salutis causa rei familiaris commoda neglegenda: vices atque aedificia incendi oportere ..."* His translation was so quick and fluent that there was a general gasp from the class and even Mrs Grain looked astonished. She had never heard anyone speak Latin

50

like this before. It was almost as it must have sounded when the Romans were nattering to each other in old Italy.

"*Quid est rei?*" asked Orcon, finally, realizing that he was creating something of a stir.

"*Quid est …?* You mean, what is the matter?" asked Mrs Grain, her eyes bulging in astonishment.

"*Sane,*" said Orcon, smoothly, meaning: "yes".

"Nothing is the matter," said Mrs Grain. "It's just – well, your translation is so good!"

Orcon smiled smugly and said, "*Mihi procedum est.*"

"Oh, yes, yes indeed, do go on Orcon," said Mrs Grain, holding her bun as if it might drop off with amazement. "Your Latin is simply excellent. I have never heard anything like it."

Orcon continued, droning on about legions, light-armed troops and auxiliaries who all seemed constantly to be doing mysterious things like "entrenching their camp" or "leaving the higher ground". He also happily whizzed through all the "having beens" that seem to crop up in Latin texts like mushrooms in an early morning field.

Finally Mrs Grain had to call a halt. She shook her head in amazement. "Asquith Minor?" she said, who was sitting next to Orcon. "Your turn."

With a great deal of whispered help from Orcon, Asquith Minor excelled at translating, leaving Mrs Grain spellbound and asking if he'd had extra tuition in the holidays. "And Sheila?"

Knowing that Sheila would take ages even to translate "and", Susan continued to whisper her theory.

"Maybe he's from outer space!" she said.

Tom and Miles stared at her and shuddered.

"What do you mean, outer space?"

"Outerum spacum, you wallies," she said, crossly. "Out there. In the sky. Mars, Jupiter, Uranus – you know."

"Spacum takes the subjunctive after a perfect participle," said Miles, grinning.

Susan glared at him and turned back to her book. But Tom felt shivers going up and down his spine. Outer space! What a terrible idea! And yet it all fitted. Orcon's clothes were so weird. They were made of a peculiar material without any seams or stitching; even his gloves didn't look as if anyone had knitted them; they seemed to have been stamped out in three woolly dimensions. And Orcon couldn't have been brought up in England or even Europe because he was, well, so foreign, even though he did speak English. And even in darkest Peru they'd never eat pepperpots or use carrots as knives and forks. And those staring eyes, those laser beams ...

He glanced at Miles. But Miles seemed to have taken no notice and was busy looking up the words he might need for the sentence he'd estimated was his, muttering "Cohort – war engine – hillock" to himself. Needless to say he'd chosen the sentence just before the one he got and, much to his fury, failed dismally. He was still in a bad temper at tea.

"Outer space!" he said, angrily buttering a piece of bread. "You two must be mentally ill. My dad –" who was a doctor – "is always seeing patients who believe in outer space. They think their television sets are being tapped by Martians. It's complete rubbish. They're schizophrenics."

"Or are they?" asked Susan, aggressively. "Maybe

52

they know something we don't." She stuffed a large jam sandwich into her mouth, leaving a ring of red around her lips.

"Oh, lipstick!" said Miles. "And you've put it on just for me! How touching."

"I have not!" said Susan, licking it away. "I would never wear make-up in a million years. Men don't wear make-up so why should women?"

"It would get in their beards and go all yucky," said Tom, thoughtfully.

"Ugh!" said Susan. Just thinking about it made her feel ill. "Can't we talk about something else?"

"What's that geography prep about?" interrupted Simon, who'd just come in from swimming with a crowd of other children, their hair glued wetly to their foreheads and all smelling slightly of chlorine. His hands were white and puckered and his nails looked soft and pliable from spending too long in the water. "How are we supposed to measure the weather?"

"We could always stick Mr Roy on the roof and then take him and squeeze him every night to find out what the rainfall was," suggested Miles.

"He's wet enough already," said Simon as he reached over for the jam. "By the way, anyone know how many Blue Peter presenters it takes to change a lightbulb?"

"Dunno," said Susan.

"Two. One to show you how it's done and another to show a lightbulb that was changed earlier!"

They laughed. "Come on, let's have a game of snooker. We've just got time before maths," said Tom. "Coming Simon?"

"No, I want more tea."

Snooker, sadly, was not much of a game at Burlap Hall

since there were only nine red balls, no yellow or black, and all the cues had lost their tips. The green baize surface of the table, used by generations of pupils to do their prep on, was covered in old inkstains. Miles always said Steve Davis would have a fit if he saw it. But in the games room there were a couple of boys fooling round with the balls on the table already, so they left, with Susan muttering that snooker and darts were only ever played by men and that it was all wrong.

"Well there are *some* advantages to being a girl," said Tom. "At least you don't have to go to war. All you have to do is knit uniforms and polish the bullets and so on."

"Polish the bullets!" said Susan, turning on him. "I've never heard anything li—"

"Well, it's better than being captured by the enemy and then interrogated," said Tom. He put on a foreign accent. "So you von't talk vill you?"

"How many enemy interrogators does it take to change a lightbulb?" asked Susan, smiling suddenly.

"Silence!" snapped back Miles, quick as a flash. "It is *ve* who ask ze questions!"

Susan laughed. "Let's go to the computer room and see if there are any games lying round."

They wandered down the corridor but just as they were about to go inside they noticed Sara, one of the younger pupils, staring intently at the panelling by the door. She looked as if she was unscrewing something. But on closer inspection she was carving the wood-work with a sharp pen-knife.

"What *are* you doing!" said Susan, peering over her shoulder. "You're writing something! 'Mr Fox is a complete ner …'"

"You can't chisel that into the panelling!" said Miles.

Sara didn't listen. She just continued with a glazed look over her face as she chipped out the final "d".

"Stop it!" said Miles. "You'll get a million detentions if anyone finds out it's you!"

But Sara didn't seem to hear. She was in a world of her own.

"Talk to us!" said Tom loudly, pulling her away. "You'll get into terrible trouble. I mean we all know he's a nerd, but it's one thing to know and another to etch it into the woodwork for everyone to see – it's mad!"

As Tom shook her, Sara woke up. She rubbed her eyes. "Stop it," she said. "Let go of me. I'm not doing anything."

"Not doing anything? What do you mean?" said Susan. "You're just half-way to being expelled, that's all!"

"Look," said Miles, pointing to the panelling.

Sara turned to the wall and started to read. She turned to them accusingly and then, as they looked back at her, she became aware of the knife in her hand. Her eyes grew to the size of saucers.

"*I* did *that*?" she said, horrified. "I must be mad! What made me ...?" Then a look of realization crept over her face. "It was that horrible new boy ... Orcon!" she said, suddenly. "I went into the computer room to do some computer prep and Orcon and Asquith Minor were in there and they said I couldn't use the computers and ... a ..." She started to cry. Susan put her arm round her. "Cheer up. We'll get some sandpaper and smooth it down. No one one will know. Go on."

"Then I sat down at one of the other computers –

55

but – but Orcon said I wasn't allowed in there. And – and – Asquith Minor said they were doing something secret. And I said I'd tell on them, and then Orcon asked how old I was ... and then ..." She burst out sobbing. "He had these horrible eyes, these horrible rays, and he told me to go outside and carve 'Mr Fox is a complete nerd' into the woodwork – and I did! I couldn't help myself! Oh, what am I going to do?"

At this moment Mr Carstairs walked briskly by. "Going to wrestle with the bits and bytes, eh?" he said, jovially. "Jolly good. Stepping into the future. One small step for mankind ... the world of communications – so exciting! Soon the world will be one great village, all countries speaking to each other through computers!"

"And all of space communicating with all the other planets, too, sir," said Tom, gloomily, while Miles and Susan pressed up against the panelling to prevent Mr Carstairs from seeing the message etched into the wood.

"I wouldn't be surprised," said Mr Carstairs, thoughtfully. "I wouldn't be surprised."

"It's all I can do to get the computer to communicate with me," said Miles. "I don't think I'm cut out for the world of bits and bytes."

"Nonsense," said Mr Carstairs, encouragingly. "I tell you what – get that new boy, Orcon, to help you with anything you don't understand. He's a genius. Ah – but of course, you already know that, don't you ..." he added, remembering the recent homework. "Still, there's no doubt he knows more about computers than – even than I!"

As he passed on, Miles muttered, "That wouldn't be too difficult, frankly," while Sara burst out crying again with all the sobs she'd been stifling while Mr Carstairs was talking to them.

"Look, forget this happened, right?" said Susan to Sara. "We'll get rid of the carving somehow – and in future, just stay out of Orcon's way."

"Thanks, Susan," said the girl, sobbing pathetically. "I'll give you one of my special lipsticks, if you want. You've been really nice."

"Lipsti —" Susan almost had a fit. But, as Miles gave her a kick, she managed to calm down. "Er – thanks a lot – maybe another time. Lipstick!" she exploded, when Sara was out of earshot. Then she turned to the two boys. "Now come on, you guys, we're going to go right in there to see what's going on."

The mention of lipstick had made her so furious that, with a toss of her red frizzy hair, she would have dared do anything. Angrily, she pushed open the door of the computer room and strode in.

Asquith Minor and Orcon were sitting in front of one of the computers, shaking with laughter. On the screen flickered a complicated drawing made up of wheels, circles, tracks and cars. Asquith Minor was at the keyboard but Orcon was giving him instructions about which buttons to press.

"How did you learn to do this stuff?" Asquith Minor was asking Orcon. "Is your father a computer expert – or an architect?"

"Oh, no. It's easy for me," said Orcon. "Now press that key and then this ..."

"Brilliant!" said Asquith Minor as a new diagram sprang on to the screen. "We'll have super fun on these dodgems! Old Fox won't know what's hit him!"

At that moment Orcon turned and spotted the trio standing by the door. He immediately reached over to the keyboard and, slamming his woolly fist on to it, switched the whole thing off.

"What are you doing here?" he piped, angrily.

"What are *you* doing?" said Susan, striding forward. "And what do you mean by playing that horrible trick on Sara! You could have got her expelled."

Both Asquith Minor and Orcon creased up with laughter. "None of your business," said Asquith Minor. "This is secret, anyway. You're not allowed to look at it!"

Miles, meanwhile, had sneaked around the side of the computer and was looking surreptitiously at bits of paper that Asquith Minor and Orcon had already printed out. While the others were arguing, he silently slipped a couple of pages inside his jacket.

"Why not?" Tom was saying. "Don't be stupid!"

"Because!" said Asquith Minor, irritatingly.

"Because!" echoed Orcon. Then he added, "Because, if you do, I'll get Sara and Arthur to do some other things – even worse than what I've told them to do already."

Susan stopped, anxiously. "That's blackmail!" she said. "You can't do that!"

"We can do anything we like!" said Asquith Minor, sticking his thumbs in his ears and waggling his fingers. "Orcon's got special powers! So ner!"

"Let's go," said Miles, winking at the others and signalling to his jacket. Realizing he'd got more information, Tom and Susan left, feigning sulky reluctance.

"Come on, quick! Before they find the papers are missing!" Miles raced down the corridor, out of the front door and into the sunshine. "They won't find us in the woods!"

The children rushed ahead, past three workmen who were in the middle of trying to lay the foundations for the science block. One was studying a huge architectural plan, another was measuring the ground, while another looked on, leaning languidly against a pile of bricks.

"So if this is going to be the lavatory ..." one was saying, scratching his head. "Laboratory," interrupted the other. "It's a special kind of lavatory." "All right. Lavoratory," conceded the other. "Then this 'ere's got to be the study room. Then over there ..." he said, pointing to a shrubbery, "that's got to be where all the chemicals are stored, which has got to be specially sealed up and fire-proofed."

"No," said a third, who was wearing a greasy woollen cap. "*That's* the lab and the room for the chemicals is over *here*. You've got these plans the wrong way round."

"Are you trying to tell me I don't know where North is?" asked the other.

The third builder joined in, licking his finger and holding it up to the wind. "North's over there," he said.

"Look, mate, you don't find North like that. That's how you tell where the wind's coming from," said the first. "No, you find North by waiting till the sun goes down and wherever it goes down is East and then you go from there."

"Isn't it West?" The first one frowned. "Look, any of you got a compass?"

"Left it back at the works," said the first.

"Better go back and find it," said the second.

"You drive, Bill, I'll look for it when we get there and Alf can drive back."

"So who's going to stay here then, and wait for you?" said Alf.

"That's a point," said Bill. And they started discussing it all again.

"British workmen!" said Susan, when they had found a particularly shady, bushy spot in the woods. "I mean workpersons! They're not like this in the States, back West!"

"'Now, where's West, eh?'" said Miles, parodying the men.

"Left of North, and right of South," said Tom. "Now, let's see what you got."

They settled down under a tree and Miles got out the papers. They all looked, craning over Miles' shoulders.

"Hey, look! It's a Big Wheel!" said Tom. He could just make out the outline on the graph paper. It had little cars hanging from the sides, with people in them. At the bottom was a design for a small hut with "Tickets" written on it.

"And a roundabout! And a coconut shy!" said Susan.

"And a ghost train!" said Miles. "What on earth can they be up to?"

"And what," added Tom, "did Asquith Minor mean by Orcon's 'special powers'?"

At the mention of Orcon's special powers, a silence fell over them. The sun was slowly setting and the distant outline of a late afternoon moon hung above them through the trees. It didn't look as pretty and romantic as usual. It looked sinister and haunting, as if it were watching them. Tom's glance flickered from the moon to the school, just visible through the leaves. What connection was there, he wondered, between the mysterious creature who'd arrived at Burlap Hall, and the huge world of space? Suddenly he could imagine the earth being seen from the moon and he realized, in the general scheme of things, how absolutely miniscule and insignificant he and his friends all were. It made him feel oddly depressed. He didn't want to go back to the school, a place that now seemed evil, trapped in Orcon's sinister web. He wanted to stay out here in the woods, free as the trees and the birds, with no anxieties about homework, exams or sinister spaceboys to worry about.

CHAPTER FIVE

There was a hum of voices from the senior common room where Mr Fox had summoned the teachers for an urgent meeting to discuss Clive Nutter's dreaded visit. It was a comfortable but shabby room. The springs were starting to burst through the faded chintz covers of the fat old chairs; the ageing Turkish carpet was almost as bald as Mr Fox himself and featured patches the texture of an ancient tennis ball. Old copies of the National Geographic magazine and syllabuses from before the war lay on the scratched, varnished tables.

Mr Carstairs and Signor Ruzzi were heatedly debating whether the computer would ever replace the musician in the concert-hall; Mr Roy and Miss Shepherd discussed the ins and outs of vegetarianism and animal liberation; Mrs Grain was silent, busy correcting homework in her neat rounded hand with phrases like: "I think not!", "Give examples", "sp" and "repetition" and "You can do better than this!"

Mixed with the musty smell of old pipe tobacco was a strong aroma of black coffee – on these occasions Signor Ruzzi always took it on himself to make what he called "real" coffee from Italy. Mr Fox would much have preferred unreal, since the smell alone made his stomach turn, but he never risked falling out with the music teacher who was quite liable to flounce off and refuse to teach, threaten to kill himself or, worst of all, burst into floods of Italian tears – which was extremely embarrassing for all concerned.

When he was certain that everyone was present, Mr Fox rose from the most comfortable chair in the room and cleared his throat. When that had no effect, he clapped his hands loudly and then, in the ensuing silence, he tugged pompously at the lapels of his coat; a slight tearing sound gave the sign that the tweed was on its last legs and he released his hands swiftly.

"I think you know why I have gathered you here this afternoon," he began. "You all know of our friend Mr Clive Nutter."

At the very mention of the name a general furious burbling ran round the room. Even Mrs Grain made a face – but, Mr Fox realized, it could have been because at that moment she had taken a sip of Signor Ruzzi's special brew.

"He has written to complain of our lack of science facilities – and, as you know, that situation is in the process of being rectified. The building of the new science block is well in hand, Mr Carstairs has surpassed himself with his computer studies course and I trust we will be able to keep Nutter's criticisms in that respect at bay. But," he continued, "I'm afraid that Clive Nutter is combining his inspection of our science facilities with a general inspection of our academic standards – to check that we are up to what he describes as the 'minimum standards required by his department'."

"Minimum standards!" Signor Ruzzi almost exploded like a bomb. "At Burlap Hall our standards are the very highest!" His voice rose to a squawk. "Highest, highest, highest! Molto highest! Highestissimo! We are – how you say? – the peach of the cream! Top-tip! The dog's whiskers! We are – we are – beezneeze!"

Mrs Grain turned, holding her bun in surprise. "What was that? Business?"

"We're the business!" chimed in Mr Carstairs, slapping his thigh. "That's what we are. We're def!"

"What?" said Mr Roy.

"No, not busy-ness," said Signor Ruzzi. "We are – um —" He pointed to his knees and then swooped his hands around, making a buzzing sound before slapping himself on his moustache and saying "Oow!" followed by "Beezneeze!"

"Bees' knees!" said Miss Shepherd, clapping her hands. "Oh, indeed, we certainly are. Burlap Hall shines like a star in God's firmament."

Inwardly, Mr Fox groaned to himself. He sometimes wondered if he wasn't worrying too much about his pupils' behaviour when Nutter paid his visit. They'd probably be fine; it was his staff who might be the problem. Although he knew they were reliable, conscientious and had their pupils' best interests at heart, what would Nutter make of them? He dreaded to think. He clapped his hands once again.

"What I must emphasize is that Clive Nutter's jealousy of my standing goes back a long way. His plan, I imagine, is to oust me from my post and run this school himself. Now, of course, you may feel that the school would be run better under Mr Nutter ..."

Mr Roy shook his head vigorously. "That man should be exterminated," he said. "He believes in corporal punishment. When I taught with him, many years ago, he delighted in beating pupils. He ruled with a rod of iron and a reign of terror."

"Corporal punishment!" Miss Shepherd looked shocked. "But that's against the European Court's rulings!"

Mrs Grain turned on her. "My dear, Clive Nutter is no respecter of anyone's laws but his own. I've heard from my friends that not only does he believe in corpo-

64

ral punishment for the pupils, he believes in corporal punishment for the teachers, too! So if you don't bring your pupils up to a certain standard, you're given six of the best! In front of the school!"

Miss Shepherd put her hands over her face and started crying. "The monster!" she wailed.

"And I've heard he's even threatened parents!" added Mr Roy. "Mr Nutter is a sadist!"

"He must have come from a very, very troubled home," sobbed Miss Shepherd. "Very troubled indeed."

Mr Fox clapped his hands once more. "Let us not waste valuable time on sympathy for Mr Nutter," he said, coldly. "Let us look at the realities of the situation. I want you all to seek out the star pupils in your classes and make sure they answer any questions Nutter asks. If necessary, you can stand behind Nutter mouthing the answers. It may not be ethical, but sometimes deceit and villainy must be answered by deceit and villainy. And we are, I am afraid, at his mercy."

Mr Carstairs was quick to get a word in. "There's no doubt about who I'd rate as star pupil in my computer class. It's Orcon – er – I don't know his surname. He's a genius. I'm thinking of entering him for a computer competition called Bits, Bytes, Bauds and Pixcels – it's sponsored by the computer magazine, *DATA! DATA!*"

Mr Roy agreed. "An odd boy and not altogether a very attractive personality, I have to say, but his grasp of geography is incredible. He seems to know everything about our planet. And other planets, too."

"I gather his maths is extraordinary," said Miss Shepherd, "although his cookery and crafts are not exactly inspired. But somehow I doubt that Clive Nutter is interested in cookery and crafts."

Signor Ruzzi shook his head dismally. "This Orcon. I agree. Technically he is a young prodigy. Better, perhaps, than Mozart himself. But there is no soul to his playing. There is no ..." – he slapped himself on the chest – "*heart*! You see," he added, looking meaningfully at Mr Carstairs, "there is more to life than technical ability."

"I doubt," said Mrs Grain wryly, "that Clive Nutter would notice any lack of heart. Certainly Orcon's Latin is remarkable. He can talk as we are talking now – in Latin! And his French is – *parfait*!"

Mr Fox still looked worried. "Although I'm delighted he has turned out so well, we can't rely on just one pupil to give a good impression of the whole school. You must find some other budding geniuses. Or if you can't find them, you must make them. Just temporarily, mind. Time for a quick work-spurt, I'd say. And now, let us turn to the happier topic of sports day. Mr Carstairs, you have some ideas, I gather?"

Mr Carstairs' ideas for sports day were, inevitably, a great deal more grandiose than most of the teachers were prepared for. He wanted it to be an all-day event; it was reduced to two hours. He wanted a relay race to Lanchester and back; it was agreed that this should be cut down to twice round the front lawn. Instead of the best of ten tries for the long and high jumps, he reluctantly had to concede to the best of three; the only thing he refused to give in on was the teachers' sack race.

"The whole idea of sport is that it encourages everyone to take part. It's a team effort," he argued. "How can we teachers stand back and expect just the kids to take part? It denies the spirit of the thing."

Surprisingly Mr Fox agreed, which made it difficult

for the teachers to protest – but only because he knew he was going to be twenty miles away at the time, bidding for a set of old school text-books at a local auction. (He also had his eye on some rather fine bottles of port that were coming up for sale as well.) There was no way Mr Fox would ever be seen dressed in a sack – although some might say anything would be an improvement on his usual wardrobe.

Despite this, the meeting broke up in a friendly way. Signor Ruzzi didn't even seem to notice when Mr Fox refused a second cup of coffee. The threat of the school inspection had brought everyone closer together. As Mrs Grain commented, the atmosphere was like it must have been in the war. "Except," as she rightly pointed out, "in the war it was the Germans. Today, it's Clive Nutter."

Mr Fox, however, had more to contend with than he realized. Because while he was addressing the teachers, a small thin figure with a big head sparsely covered with wispy hair, buttoned up to the neck and wearing thick woolly gloves, was at that very moment whispering outside Mr Fox's study to Asquith Minor who clutched a set of papers under his arm.

After a lot of giggling and looking around, Asquith Minor tiptoed into the study and peered at the desk on which lay another collection of papers – plans for the science block. Swiftly, he swapped these with his own papers and tiptoed out again, carrying the original science block plans.

Had Mr Fox had very sharp eyes, he would have spotted that the plans now on his desk were very different from the ones he'd left there that morning.

But Mr Fox did not have very sharp eyes.

The friendship between Asquith Minor and Orcon had grown out of the incident at Leisure Music. Orcon was grateful to Asquith Minor for protecting him against the taunts of the other pupils; Asquith Minor was grateful to Orcon for getting him off the hook by playing the piano so brilliantly. Since then the pair had become inseparable, partly because both possessed the same streak of mischievous devilry. Orcon also appreciated Asquith Minor's help in a number of little ways.

There had been the embarrassing moment at cricket when Orcon, who was fielding, thought that it was his job to catch everything from falling leaves, butterflies and even the cricket bat. A particularly successful batsman was astonished when, on throwing his bat happily into the air after hitting a six, it was snatched by a leaping Orcon who raced off with it and hid it in the bushes. Asquith Minor had sat down with Orcon that night and patiently explained the rules of the game.

Then there was his voice. Although he might be a wizard on the piano keys, when it came to singing hymns at assembly, Orcon was completely confused. He would twiddle away inside his shirt and sometimes the voice of a shrieking soprano would emerge; it could equally well be a booming bass. On one occasion he opened his mouth and nothing came out but the sound of syncopated drums. Asquith Minor advised him to forget singing and simply mime the words.

His sleeping habits were peculiar, too. He needed sleep, certainly; but he only needed half an hour. Then he would get up and start roaming round the school. Asquith Minor got him out of trouble twice by inventing excuses for him when this occurred and eventually persuaded him it was better simply to lie in bed staring into the darkness.

For his part, Asquith Minor was extremely impressed by Orcon's powers. Any small child who dared to laugh at Orcon for his mistakes would soon regret it. After only a couple of weeks he had organized a small army of slaves consisting of children younger than himself – children who were too frightened of Orcon to object. After all, *they* didn't want to end up like poor Arthur Mitsford – or any of the other children he had hypnotized as punishment for not going along with him. It had only taken a couple more examples of his hypnotic strength – Simon, just a month younger than Orcon, had been obliged to flick pieces of ink-soaked paper pellets at Mr Roy, and Rosemary had been forced to put a drawing pin on Signor Ruzzi's music stool – to convince everyone younger than Orcon that what he said, went.

Tom and Miles, when their bath night coincided with Orcon's, were astonished to witness the extent to which his reign of terror had grown. Their baths were sufficiently close to Orcon's for them to witness, even before his arrival in the bathrooms, small boys already busy, polishing the bathtub, breathing on the taps and rubbing them till they glistened; some were shaking out the bathmat and fluffing it up, others were starting to fill the bath with water, using a thermometer to get exactly the correct temperature for the little dictator.

Not wanting to draw too much attention to themselves, Tom and Miles got undressed slowly and submerged themselves quietly in the warm water. Miles started to soap himself – and then made a quick count of the hairs on his chest. "Hang on," he said, "I'm missing one! Oh, no. There it is. Phew!"

When Orcon arrived, he was immediately surrounded by another little group of slaves who jostled for a place near him and kept asking him if he wanted anything. He shook his big head imperiously and then prepared to get undressed. Not that he really did get undressed. He took off most of his clothes, true, but he prepared to get into his bath while wearing a scarf tied round his neck, a vest, pants, thick woollen socks and gloves.

As he took off his outer clothes, he handed his jacket, shirt, trousers and jersey to the various young lackeys. But before he got into the bath he snapped his woolly fingers. They made a feeble, furry sound.

Arthur Mitsford jumped to attention. "Yes, sir?" he asked, meekly.

"A dryer. I need something to dry my underclothes when I get out," said Orcon in a lordly way.

"Why don't you take them off before you get in?" asked Arthur, in a scared kind of way. Then, suddenly remembering, he quickly added, "Er – O Mighty Ruler Who Shall be Obeyed."

Orcon turned on him furiously. "Did anyone ask you for your opinion?"

Arthur was silent. Through the steam that rose from Orcon's bath Tom could see he was starting to cry.

"Did they?"

Arthur shook his head sadly.

"Answer me, you moron!" yelled Orcon.

"No," replied Arthur in a whisper.

"No, what?" screamed Orcon.

"No, O Mighty Ruler Who Shall Be Obeyed," whispered Arthur.

"Do you want to go and put a frog in Miss

Shepherd's bed, by any chance?" roared Orcon.

"No, O Mighty Ruler Who Shall Be Obeyed," said Arthur, choking back a sob.

"Then do as I say!" screamed Orcon. His face was contorted with fury. "Get me something to dry my clothes!"

Arthur scuttled off like a beetle, glad to get out of the sight of his tyrannical master, and Orcon, dressed in vest, gloves, socks and scarf, delicately stepped into the bath.

Miles and Tom craned their necks to watch. As Orcon reached to take the soap from a little boy who held it out to him, his vest lifted up slightly and revealed completely smooth white skin underneath. Nothing surprising, perhaps, about that – except that the sharp-eyed Miles spotted something was missing. A belly button.

"That means only one thing," he said, whispering in an awed voice to Tom. "He's not human!"

Tom stared but Orcon had turned back and his tummy was no longer visible. What he did notice, however, were a couple of bumps under Orcon's vest that looked like little knobs. "Those must be what he twiddles when he wants to change his language," he said to Miles, pointing.

"And have you noticed," whispered Miles, peering intently over the side of the bath like an otter, "that he never goes to the lavatory? I think he's all sealed up like a plastic Actionman."

Tom didn't want to think about this aspect of Orcon. But he couldn't help asking, "But he does eat our food. So where does it go?"

Miles shook his head. "Perhaps he unscrews part of himself at night and then it just falls out and he chucks it all away in a bin. After all, he was just about to eat that pepperpot until he realized something was wrong."

Tom thought about it. True, he didn't seem to chew his food; he just put it in like you might put a letter into a postbox. Tom imagined his meals rattling around in a kind of waste-bin inside him, just waiting to be emptied. It gave him the creeps.

At that moment Orcon turned sharply in his bath.

"I feel as if someone is staring at me!" he said imperiously to another small boy who was waiting by his master with the soap.

"Where?" asked the little boy, terrified of being spoken to by Orcon.

"There!" said Orcon, reaching out and pointing in the direction of Tom and Miles' baths.

Miles immediately turned on the hot tap and started singing in a loud voice as he washed himself busily. The little boy gaped and finally said to Orcon, "It's only a couple of boys having baths."

"Hmph," said Orcon. "Ah – Arthur. Have you got something to dry me with?"

Arthur produced a hair dryer he had found in some girl's room and was about to plug it into a socket outside the door when Orcon screamed, "You fool! Are you trying to kill me? Don't you know that electricity travels along water? Unplug that thing at once and get out of here! Get me a hot towel! For that blunder I'll make you dance on the tables at supper!" Arthur rushed off again. Orcon got out of his bath, dripping furiously, and the dictator and his entourage swept from the room.

Miles looked at Tom. "Did you see that!" he said, appalled.

"What?"

"When he pointed to us, you could see the bit where his hand joins his wrist – and there were *scales*!"

"Like a fish?"

"Yes!" said Miles. "Like a fish! Ugh!" He paused, worriedly. "Look, we can't just stand by and let him take over the whole of the lower school. I know Arthur Mitsford's really stupid but it's not his fault. And Orcon is just – well, terrorizing him as well as the others."

"There's only one thing we can do," said Tom, as he stepped out of the now luke-warm bath, rather wishing, like Orcon, that he had a hot towel waiting for him. "We'll have to confront him."

"Isn't that a bit risky?" said Miles. "I mean – I don't want to be made to do anything ..."

"He can't touch us," said Tom. "He's only got power over people younger than him. And we're too old."

The following day was sports day – or rather, sports afternoon as it had become. It was gorgeous summer weather and the grounds of Burlap Hall were at their best. The horse-chestnuts were in full flower, candles of pink and white on huge ancient trees around the lawn. True, the grass was covered with daisies, but it really only made the scene even prettier, and as Mr Fox ambled down the gravel path at the side of the school where the builders were working, even the prospect of Clive Nutter seemed less daunting on a day like this. A couple of days ago he'd given the builders the second set of plans that the architect had sent him and he wanted to know how they were getting on.

He found them on site, sitting down with their shirts

off, having a cup of tea and staring at the sky. They looked suspiciously as if they were just preparing to sunbathe but, Mr Fox supposed, it *was* just possible they'd taken their shirts off because they were preparing for a day of back-breaking work. Unlikely, of course, but possible.

"Hello, guv," said Bill, getting up reluctantly. "Glad you came by. These plans. They don't make sense."

"Don't make sense!" Mr Fox's brief period of serenity ended abruptly and he felt like banging his head against a brick wall – except, at the rate those builders were working, there wouldn't be a brick wall to bang his head against until some time the following year. "I got them last week from the architect! I've paid for them! They're the second stage. Not that you've finished the first stage, I see," he said, despairingly, as he looked round. What on earth had they been doing for the past couple of weeks? Apart from a few lines of string pegged out on the ground, nothing seemed to have been achieved at all.

"Well, you see, guv," said Alf, "these here plans aren't for a lavatory. They're for a funfair."

"A FUNFAIR!" roared Mr Fox. "A FUNFAIR! And for the last time I do *not* want a lavatory built here. We have perfectly adequate toilet facilities in the main building."

"He means your lavoratory," explained the third builder. "What you call your lab."

"That's better," said Mr Fox. "But what do you mean, a funfair? Are you drunk? Or just stark raving mad?"

Rather than try to explain, Alf decided it would be easier to show him.

"Look here," he said, spreading the plans out on the

74

grass. "This here's a big wheel. And over here you've got your dodgems. And there's a roundabout here. And if I'm not much mistaken this thing here's a Black Hole of Death – or something of the kind. Look, you can see the little cars and people. Looks a good ride, mind."

Mr Fox reeled. He thought he would blow into several pieces with rage. He'd read of people suddenly exploding into flames – spontaneous combustion, it was called – and no one knew why it happened. Now, however, he was able to provide the answer. It was because these people were driven absolutely up the wall – but again, what wall? – by idiot workmen who didn't know one end of a plan from another.

"JUST GET ON WITH IT, will you?" he said. "I don't want to hear any more about it. Dodgems, roundabouts, black holes ..." He shook his head so vigorously that the piece of hair he had carefully plastered over his balding head flew into the air and he had to catch it and smarm it back. "These plans have been drawn up *especially* by an architect. Heard of architects? People who train for years and years to design buildings. These plans have been *especially* drawn up by an architect and they are the plans for our NEW SCIENCE BLOCK! And talking of blocks, the only blocks around here will be the three I've knocked off your three shoulders if you don't snap to it! Now get on with it."

He turned on his heel and left, stamping furiously on the ground at each step, rather proud of his final remarks. It signified that he possessed, he thought, a certain wry irony.

Bill scratched his head and looked at the others.

"Well, I suppose we'd better do as he says," he said, resignedly. "Bang goes our sunbathing. And gawd only knows what kind of temper he'll be in when he sees the result."

Wearily, they started mixing the concrete.

"Scales?" said Susan, as Tom and Miles told her their news that morning. Their class had been deputed to organize the grounds for sports day – or afternoon. Some of their friends were marking out the lines for the relay race on the lawn; others were erecting the poles for the high-jump; in a corner Mr Carstairs supervised the careful digging of the stretch for the long-jump which was to be filled with sand. Endless trails of kids trooped out carrying cups, plates, flags, poles and all the sports day paraphernalia that hadn't been seen since the same day last year. "No belly button? He bathed in his *socks*?" Then she laughed and pulled the marking machine towards her, making a wet white line on the blades of grass. "Are you sure?"

"Sure," said Miles. "Or my name's Napoleon."

"Since when?" asked Tom, in mock surprise. "This is all so sudden. All I can say is, keep away from Waterloo, whatever you do. It will be the end of an illustrious career."

"Oh, do shut up, you two," snapped Susan. "Now do you *really* mean this? If so it's serious."

Tom and Miles looked at each other, sighing.

"And Tom says we've got to confront him," said Miles, taking the machine from her and dragging it away to make the line more distinct. Some of the whitewash spilled over on to Tom's shoes. "Watch it!" he said, wiping the sides on the grass.

"Well, if what you say is true, then," said Susan, "he must be checked."

"No, his skin was quite plain. No patterns at all, just

76

scales," said Miles.

Susan looked to heaven. But Tom interrupted, "And under his vest he had these funny bumps that looked like knobs – you know how when he wants to be good at anything he just twiddles something under his shirt as if he's kind of tuning in to something."

The friends were silent for a moment. From the school came the familiar sounds of Signor Ruzzi's music class – tinkling piano followed by low moans from the Italian. "More feeeleeng!" he was saying, "From the heart! Now – again!" A clattering of pots and pans from the kitchens meant that lunch was being prepared; a screech of chalk from a blackboard near an open window sent shivers down Tom's spine. Mr Carstairs was calling, "Who's got the rosettes?" and "Where's the starting gun?" Then the sounds were interrupted by Mr Fox's car starting up and slowly rumbling down the drive. The headmaster stuck his head out of the window as he passed. "Have a successful sports day!" he shouted cheerfully to the children, as he revved up and roared out of the school gates.

It was at this moment that Orcon passed Tom, Miles and Susan on the lawn. He had an unpleasant grin on his face. In one hand he held a bunch of red rosettes with First Prize written on them. In the other was a bunch of blue and yellow rosettes with Second and Third Prize written on them.

"Ah, Orcon, we were just talking about you." Susan, as usual, was tackling the problem head on. Tom, who had got cold feet about the whole idea of confronting aliens, tried to change the subject.

"What are you doing this afternoon? Taking part in any events?" he asked the creature in as friendly a way possible.

Orcon stopped. "Athletics are not my strong point, as you know," he said, rather sarcastically, in his high, thin voice. "I have been deputed to assess the scores. And what are you doing?"

Susan tried to butt in but Tom hurriedly interrupted in an attempt to keep the conversation light.

"Oh, me, I'm hoping to do well in the long-jump. And Miles is a great high-jumper. And Susan's in the relay race," he replied.

Susan scowled. "We weren't talking about that," she said, crossly to Tom. "We were talking about aliens. And knobs under vests."

That had torn it. Tom noticed Orcon's woolly hand freezing round the rosettes at the word "alien".

"And didn't you say aliens had *scales* under their gloves?" continued Susan, turning to Miles. "And I was particularly interested in what you were saying about the absence of belly buttons. In fact, we were just going to compare belly buttons when you came along," she added to Orcon. Then she lifted her jersey and pulled down her waistband with a slight titter. "Like mine? Neat, isn't it. Not bumpy like some people's."

"Mine's not bumpy," said Miles, revealing his. Susan peered at it.

"Ugh, it's got bits of fluff in it," she said, staring. "Put it away."

"It's where I keep my notes in exams," said Miles, laughing.

"So that's why you always fluff them," said Tom, trying to maintain the light-hearted tone. But Orcon didn't laugh.

"OK, Orcon," added Susan, turning to their fellow-pupil who was turning green with fury. "Your turn.

Then Tom'll show you his."

But Orcon's face had become even greener. He fixed them all with a deadly gaze. The rosettes dropped to the ground and his woolly hands clenched into fists.

"If you were just one day younger than me ..." he hissed threateningly, in his squeaky voice.

"But we're not!" sang Susan. "We're all older than you. Just slightly – but it makes all the difference, doesn't it? Because," she hesitated, "aliens from outer space – at least the outer space you come from – only have power over people younger than themselves. So, as we say on earth, ner!"

One glance at Orcon's horrified face showed that Susan had hit on the truth.

"Not to mention, ner-ner-ner-*ner*-ner!" echoed Tom, bravely. "You came out of the computer, didn't you? It was me who got you down here. Now why don't you go back before you create any more trouble?"

"Trouble?" said Orcon in his high-pitched voice. "Trouble? Huh! You don't know what trouble is. I suppose none of you thought that I might have – a brother? And an *older* brother, at that!"

Tom froze. Miles grew pale. Susan bravely said, "A brother! Typical! Can't even have a sister! Not just a spaceboy but sexist with it."

A crowd of children pushed past them carrying a long trestle table, unaware of the tense scene they were interrupting. But Tom noticed some of them looking worried as they passed Orcon, screwing up their eyes as if to pretend he wasn't there.

"Yes. A brother. A brother who's not only older than me but also older than *you*. A brother who would just *love* to pop down to Burlap Hall for a few weeks and have some fun. He's very bored at school back where

79

we come from. I'm sure he'd enjoy sports day. And he could do with some exercise as he's rather fat. I hope," added Orcon, "that none of you want to use the computers for the moment? Because I have rather a long and complicated piece of work to do. I hope you will excuse me."

With a contemptuous shake of his big head, he put the rosettes on the grass and walked away back to the school. Tom, Miles and Susan turned to each other in horror.

"What on earth's he going to do now?" asked Miles.

"I don't think that the expression 'on earth' is appropriate just at this minute," said Tom. "Let's follow him."

They went down to the computer room and tried the door. It was locked. And inside all they could hear was the sound of Orcon feverishly tapping the computer keys. And giggling to himself.

CHAPTER SIX

Tom, Miles and Susan waited anxiously outside the computer room.

"What do you think he's up to?" asked Susan, worriedly.

Tom shook his head. Perhaps it had been a mistake to confront him. Tom was sure aliens from outer space didn't like being confronted. A confronted alien might do anything – he might spin you away down the years so you became a chimney sweep in Victorian times; he might make you into an awful flat square like in that old Superman film and leave you whirling about in space for ever and ever; he might scoop out your brain and put another alien brain into your skull and everyone would think it was you but in fact it wouldn't be you at all. Or – Tom's mind raced through all the horrible films he'd ever seen – he might plant one of those creepy toothy creatures inside you which would pop out of your tummy like in a film he'd seen last holidays. He didn't say any of this to the others, however. He just said, "Oh, don't worry. I'm sure it'll be all right."

At that moment Asquith Minor came sauntering down the corridor carrying a bundle of poles and ropes.

"Seen Orcon?" he asked.

"He's in there," said Miles pointing to the closed door. "We're worried."

"What about?" said Asquith Minor, stopping.

"Don't you think he's weird?" said Susan. "Hasn't it crossed your mind he might be – different?"

Asquith Minor's face puckered into an angry frown.

"Well – yes, he's different. He's good fun."

There was a long pause as they all stared at each other. Asquith Minor leant the poles against the wall and was just about to turn the door knob when Susan put a hand on his arm.

"Wait," she said. "We think he's ..."

She stopped, unable to go on.

"He's from outer space," said Tom, finishing her sentence for her.

Asquith Minor stared at them unbelievingly. Then a grin spread across his face.

"Outer space?" He started to laugh. "Rubbish. He's just a weird kind of person. I like him. He's got all kinds of plans, you know ..." he added, conspiratorially, but then quickly clapped a hand over his mouth as if he'd said too much. "Sorry. It's secret. He's my best friend you know. You'd be amazed if you knew what I knew. For instance, when you burst in on us we were making plans for a ..." but he couldn't go on. He was laughing too much. "You'll see, anyway. He's a good laugh."

"But," cried Susan, "he virtually admitted to us he's an alien. Have you ever seen his feet or his hands? They're covered in scales. And he's got no belly button. And he's got knobs all over his chest! And he's got this weird power over all the little kids and he's creepy."

"Just a strong personality," said Asquith Minor. "But he *is* sensitive about his hands. And I don't blame him. He's got eczema and he has to wear gloves all the time. Scales! Honestly!"

"And he *never* goes to the lavatory," said Miles. "Either he's completely constipated or he doesn't have a bottom."

Asquith Minor scratched his head. "Well … maybe. But surely you don't count how many times people go to the lavatory, do you?"

"No, of course not, stupid," said Susan, "but you do expect just once in a while people to say they're going to the john – I mean the jane – don't you? I mean *never* is rather odd."

"I suppose it is," conceded Asquith Minor, pausing. But then he shook his head. "What the hell. I don't care. I don't believe what you say, anyway. He's a good mate of mine and I've had more fun this term than I've ever had in my life."

"How old are you?" asked Miles, suddenly.

Asquith Minor frowned. "None of your – well, who cares. Actually, I'm just a day older than Orcon."

"Exactly!" said Susan, triumphantly. "He's got no power over you. So he can't …"

But at that moment the door of the computer room opened and Orcon came out with a horrible smile on his green face. His great saucer-like eyes glowed with triumph and he was breathing deeply. He didn't notice Asquith Minor who was the other side of the door.

"Ha!" he said, standing there, his woolly hands on his hips. "Ha! Ha! And ha! again! You're in for the surprise of your life."

Tom was suddenly furious. He felt so powerless against this strange creature and it frightened him.

"Now you're going to meet my brother. He's coming down right now."

"Down from where?" said Susan.

Orcon pointed a knitted finger upwards. "Up there. You know where. In the stars. And he's not just a brother. He's my big, big brother. He's *older than you!*"

Tom couldn't restrain himself. "Take your gloves off

and show Asquith Minor what you really are!" he said, challenging him.

Orcon turned and noticed Asquith Minor with surprise. "I don't see why I should show you anything," he said. "I've got eczema. Asquith Minor knows that. I'm sensitive about it."

Tom pushed up to Orcon angrily. He really felt that if only Asquith Minor could see Orcon's hands, he'd believe them. And then Orcon would have no friends at all. It would help.

"Until your brother arrives, you can't do anything about us," he said, grabbing hold of one of Orcon's gloved hands. "Come on, let's see them!"

He pulled at the gloves but they wouldn't come off. He shoved Orcon in the chest and felt the little dials through his shirt – a horrible feeling that made him flinch. Orcon lashed out at Tom and soon they were fighting, Tom punching Orcon in the chest, on the face, and Orcon giving as good as he got until, caught by a blow from Tom, he slipped to the ground.

"It's no good," said Susan, pulling Tom off the spaceboy. "Fighting won't get you anywhere!"

Orcon struggled up off the floor. "Varmints!" he cried, "Scoundrels and villains! Thou shalt pay for this dearly, and wilst regret the day you were born, egad! A thousand curses, my voice!" he added, as he shook himself. "Thou hast impeded my speech and shalst sorely suffer!" He reached inside his shirt and started twiddling with the knobs on his chest.

"Look, Asquith Minor!" cried Tom, pointing. "Can't you see? He's twiddling those knobs we told you about!"

And Asquith Minor, staring, couldn't help but notice his friend's strange behaviour. Finally, after a series of explosive crackles, Orcon adjusted himself correctly. He banged himself on the ribs. Then he smoothed down his clothes with a cunning smile. "You'll regret this," he said, slyly. And, reaching for the handle of the computer room door, he opened it and called softly, "Porcon! I wonder if you could help me?"

And through the door marched Orcon's brother.

He was identical to Orcon in every way, from the gloves to the shoes; the only difference was that he was bigger and, clearly, older. He had the same large saucer-like eyes, the same big head, the same wispy hair. His face was the same greenish colour – but his smile was even less friendly than Orcon's. To make matters worse, he was very, very fat. Asquith Minor blinked and rubbed his eyes. How had this new boy arrived? Perhaps Tom, Miles and Susan's story had something to it after all.

"Yes?" Porcon's voice had the same high-pitched quality as his brother's.

"These lousy kids," said Orcon, pointing to Tom, Miles and Susan. "Deal with them for me, will you?" He whispered in Porcon's ear. Porcon whispered back and together they laughed.

"Later," said Porcon, rubbing his gloved hands cunningly. "Later. You'll see."

"Now, let me introduce you to my friend," said Orcon. "Asquith Minor – my brother, Porcon!"

And Porcon, with a horrid smile, held out his gloved hand.

Asquith Minor felt, deep down, immensely frightened. He didn't like the turn things had taken. If Tom, Miles and Susan were right, then now Porcon had arrived the brothers could make him do what they wanted. He shivered. He remembered what had happened to Arthur Mitsford, and he remembered how funny he'd found it when Orcon had made Sara carve "Mr Fox is a compete nerd" into the woodwork – but it wasn't so funny when there was a chance of *him* being on the receiving end of the same sinister powers. He had better, he decided, be nice to them. Very nice indeed. He roared with laughter as he shook Porcon's hand. "Great to meet you!" he said, in an over-friendly way. "Just arrived?"

Orcon looked at Porcon meaningfully. "Er – yes," said Porcon. "I was held up. I've been ill. Only just got here. Lovely school you've got here!" And then Orcon and Porcon both burst into fits of hysterical high-pitched giggles and, each taking one of Asquith Minor's arms, they set off down the corridor. They were being very friendly, thought Asquith Minor. Almost over-friendly. Trapped between them he felt less like a member of a jolly trio of mates than a prisoner being accompanied to jail by two policemen. It wasn't a nice feeling at all.

Sports day started at two o'clock. The school was in pandemonium. Kids were climbing up trees, pushing each other into the sandy long-jump and waggling the poles of the high-jump; some were climbing into the sacks intended for the teachers' sack-race and shouting, "I'm a potato! Peel me!"

The general uproar might have been something to do with the sun that beat down on the huge school lawn, like an oven with the door open. Wherever you stood, you were too hot. Even in the shade you were too hot. It was typical sports day weather – when everyone felt far too hot and bothered even to consider anything serious like a leap or a jump or a run. Even a small scamper or a limp was too much.

Mr Carstairs, standing on a chair under the chestnut tree, finally brought some order to the proceedings as he explained the arrangements and the timing of the events. Mr Roy stood nearby looking completely mad in shorts and running shoes, his pale bony knees sticking out as if this was the first time they'd ever seen the light of day and they didn't like what they saw. Miss Shepherd, in charge of the long-jump, had discovered some peculiar old white dress that made her look like a tennis star of the twenties. Mrs Grain stood behind a long table covered with plates of sandwiches and orange quarters, guarding an enormous steaming metal drum with TEA written on the side.

Signor Ruzzi had been dragged in to dispense the rosettes, but at that moment he was supervising the moving of the piano on to the lawn so that they could all sing the old school song at the end of the afternoon.

As Mr Carstairs spoke, Tom could see, out of the corner of his eye, the vast figure of Porcon, dressed in gloves, striped T-shirt, enormous shorts, long socks and running shoes. He stood alone, most children having sensibly given him a wide berth. He seemed to be taking a particular interest in Tom, gradually edging closer to him; at the same time Tom tried to hide himself deeper among the crowds of pupils and, for a moment, Porcon lost sight of him.

But Tom was exposed when he was taking part in the events themselves. The event he had been most looking forward to was the long-jump. He had always prided himself on his leaping abilities. His legs were longer than most and he expected to carry off at least this one prize, particularly when he saw the standard of the other competitors landing feebly only half-way down the sandy strip.

When it was his turn he surveyed the scene and, on being given a sign by Miss Shepherd, he started running, trying to build up speed to carry him right over the long stretch of sand. As he got closer and closer to the white line, the rows of cheering children on the sidelines became a blur of colour. He prepared himself to spring. But as he anticipated his jump, he was aware of a strange feeling. Porcon was looking at him. He turned his head briefly – and was hit by a glance from the spaceboy's eyes. They glowered bright and burning and, out of them, lashed two purple laserbeams. They grew out of the fat boy's face like poles.

It was at this very moment that Tom's foot touched the white line and he jumped. But it was no ordinary jump. Try as he might to thrust his body forward, his legs seemed to have other ideas. He leapt what seemed to be six feet into the air completely vertically like a bouncing ball and landed exactly where he had taken off, on the white line. His legs didn't seem to belong to him any more. They had a mind of their own. And the next thing they decided to do was, with a series of short bunny hops, to skip across the stretch of sand, turning the odd somersault as they did so and leaving Tom foolish and gasping at the other end.

There was uproar. The watching children burst into roars of laughter as Tom picked himself up, covered in sand. He was about to ask for another go but his ludicrous performance had spoilt any further chances. Miss Shepherd drew herself up and, with a look of fury, said, "That was a ridiculous display, Tom. You will not be allowed to take part in further events. You didn't even try! You were just clowning around! Next, please!"

Tom crawled from the long-jump area feeling choked. He'd really been looking forward to getting a rosette. He was miserable. Ambling over to the high-jump where Miles was about to take a leap over the bar, Tom suddenly spotted Porcon watching the event. Rushing over, Tom tried to warn Miles. But it was too late. Porcon was already looking at Miles as he was waiting his turn. The laser beams grew and grew out of his eyes until they fired straight into the depths of Miles' mind.

Which is why Miles, when he'd psyched himself up for the crucial leap, didn't take off like a bird but found himself running at great speed *under* the bar – and then round and round again till he collapsed in a dizzy heap. The onlookers booed and whistled – and Mr Roy immediately disqualified him from taking part in other events. Tom raced up to his friend and helped him away.

"It was Porcon!" said Miles, rubbing his head. "I felt him looking at me! It was a horrible feeling!"

"I know," said Tom, commiserating. "He did the same to me."

"Where's Susan?" asked Miles. "She'll be next, won't she?"

"She's in the relay race," said Tom. "Let's go and warn her."

They found her waiting to grab the baton from the next member of her team who was at that moment in the lead, whizzing round the lawn, panting desperately and being cheered by her team.

"I can't talk now," said Susan, her eyes fixed on the runner. "I've just *got* to concentrate. It all depends on me now."

But even though they managed to whisper a warning

to her, she couldn't resist Porcon's stare. He had come right up and glared at her. As he did so, a terrible shock went through her; her knees turned to jelly and she felt faint and sick.

And when her fellow runner dashed up, gasping for breath, and thrust the baton in Susan's hands, she tried to run. She really did try. But she couldn't. All she could do was walk. And not just walk normally, but walk with a ridiculous little wiggle in her bottom as if she were pretending to be Marilyn Monroe. All her classmates were clapping and hissing and yelling at her to get a move on, but nothing worked. She simply sauntered sexily around the lawn as each member of the other teams easily overtook her.

"What a shame, Susan!" cried Mr Carstairs as she eventually wobbled to the winning post. "You really let the team down! What a poor show! You may have thought it was funny but no one else did!"

"No! No one thought it was funny at all!" yelled Sheila, who had been in Susan's team. "It's not fair!" Two other members of the team came up to Susan as if they were about to lynch her but luckily an announcement, crackling over the loudhailer, distracted their attention.

"And now – the event you've all been waiting for – the teachers' sack race!"

Asquith Minor came up to them nervously. "I say – I…" he said. But Miles, Tom and Susan turned their backs on him. "Spacespy!" muttered Susan. "Turncoat!" whispered Miles. "Yolly yolly yellowlegs!" hissed Tom, not knowing what on earth it meant. But Asquith Minor was shocked. He even went a faint shade of yellow as if the insult had really struck home.

On the far side of the lawn, the teachers were clambering rather crossly into their sacks. Signor Ruzzi tore his the moment he jumped in, and his legs stuck out through two rips, making him look like a turkey with a moustache. Mr Roy simply disappeared completely into his sack and had to be fished out by Mrs Grain, who arranged it neatly around him; then she got into her own sack and promptly fell over. Miss Shepherd managed to wear her sack more successfully.

"Rather suits her, don't you think?" said Miles, unsympathetically. "Better than that dreadful old dress."

Soon all the teachers were lined up, Mr Carstairs wrapped in a black binbag in which he stood out as the obvious winner. And he was the only one to finish the course, the others either falling over or huffily stepping out of their bags when they realized the race was lost rather than suffer the jeers and catcalls of their pupils. He accepted the applause with great enthusiasm and jollity before clapping his hands for silence. Tom, Miles and Susan were so absorbed in the race that they had dropped their guard. They didn't notice Porcon waddling up and taking his position behind them.

"And now, before the prizes, and before tea," announced Mr Carstairs, "the old school song! Signor Ruzzi – take it away!"

Signor Ruzzi, who was sitting at the piano still dressed in his sack, raised his hands to begin. But before his fingers hit the notes Tom, Miles and Susan felt their mouths opening wide. They stared at each other wildly. They knew that something was going to come out of their mouths and they also knew it wasn't going to be the old school song. And they were right. In complete unison, they started to chant:

> "School stinks!
> Lessons pong!
> We know
> What is wrong."

In vain did they put their hands over their mouths to stop the words coming. Their vocal chords were working independently; they had no control over them at all. To their horror the verses poured out.

> "Mr Fox has smelly socks,
> Mr Roy's a pain,
> Miss Shepherd is quite barmy
> And Carstairs has no brain.

> "Signor Ruzzi's out of tune
> And Mrs Grain's a frump.
> We want to get away 'cos
> Burlap Hall's a dump."

And then Miles said loudly: "Because ... altogether now!" and then they all joined in again, now marching loudly around the lawn and yelling at the top of their voices to the astonishment of the pupils and teachers who were struck dumb by this display. "School stinks! Lessons pong! We know – *what* is wrong! Mr Fox has sm ..."

Mr Roy rushed up. He had forgotten he'd not taken his sack off, so he leapt up to them like a kangaroo, feet together and hopping madly.

"Tom, Miles, Susan! Stop this at once!" he said, trying to stand in front of them. They simply marched around him.

Mrs Grain followed. "Stop it! How dare you!" she

shrieked. Her bun had come completely adrift.

Finally Signor Ruzzi rose up from the piano and pushed his way forward. His voice was extremely loud. "Silence!" he screamed. "Out of tune I am not! Finito! End!"

The effect of his roar seemed to rouse the three friends from their trance. Their voices got slower and fainter and their marching got more and more half-hearted until it ceased altogether. Slowly, they became aware of what they'd been doing – and they emerged, horrified, from their spell.

"Cripes," whispered Miles. "What's he made us do? This is terrible!"

Susan was shaking. "I'm so sorry, I'm so sorry," she said to Signor Ruzzi, twisting her hands. "Of course you're not out of tune."

Tom shook his head, mystified. He looked imploringly at Mrs Grain. "We're dreadfully sorry. You know us. We'd never normally do that sort of thing. We don't even mean it."

The teachers, meanwhile, were all looking at each other baffled. It was completely out of character for Tom, Miles and Susan to behave like this. It wasn't as if they were saints by any means. But this was just so extraordinary.

Worse, of course, this concerted attack didn't reflect well on any of the teachers. Not only had they been insulted but the display proved they couldn't keep order when Mr Fox was away. So when Mr Carstairs said, "Right, I shall report you at once to Mr Fox when he returns," Mrs Grain looked at him questioningly. She drew him aside and whispered to him. "Do you think that's such a good idea?" she said. "I mean – with Clive Nutter coming? We don't want to worry him."

"Deal with them ourselves, that's the best," said Mr Roy, who'd joined them.

"Out of tune, my feet!" scoffed Signor Ruzzi. "Never!"

"Perhaps," murmured Miss Shepherd, "it's the heat. People do very funny things in the heat."

Miles stepped forward. "Honestly, we really are sorry. I just don't know how it happened. I promise it won't happen again. I know you'll give us detentions, but quite honestly, it was as if we were in a kind of trance – or rather, we were sort of threatened ..."

Tom and Susan nodded and both looked shame-facedly at their shoes. They felt absolutely terrible. Now Porcon had power over them, goodness knows what he'd make them do next. The whole prospect was terrifying.

Eventually Mr Carstairs spoke. "I don't know if you're aware, but Clive Nutter, the schools' inspector, is coming to visit this school next week. He is going to take a good look at not only the educational standards but also the general level of behaviour in the school. Mr Fox, as you can understand, is extremely worried about this visit."

Tom, Miles and Susan nodded. The feud between Nutter and Fox was common knowledge.

"We view what has happened most seriously," he said. "In my opinion it merits expulsion."

"Expulsion and detention," added Mrs Grain.

"Expulsion, detention and a case of slander ..." added Mr Roy.

"And damages," said Miss Shepherd.

"And to be put on the whitelist for every other school in the country!" said Signor Ruzzi.

"Blacklist," said Mr Carstairs. But as he spoke he gradually became aware that all the children in the school were listening to his every word. With an imperious gesture he signalled to Mrs Grain. "Please organize tea," he said. "This is not a sideshow!" And Mrs Grain shooed the pupils away from the scene, kids started grabbing sandwiches, spilling drinks and so on and gradually things got back to their normal chaos.

Mr Carstairs beckoned Tom, Miles and Susan and the other teachers under the chestnut tree. He faced them sternly. "If Clive Nutter forms an unfavourable opinion, there is the chance that he will take over as headmaster from Mr Fox. In the light of this, and because Mr Fox must not be made more anxious than he is already, I will not mention this to the headmaster. Instead, I shall give you all two punishments each, one of which will be no tea today and the disgrace of not attending prize-giving; the other is that singlehanded you three will, tomorrow morning, clear the entire lawn of sports day equipment and put it away."

"And then say no more about it," said Mr Roy, hastily. "Not a word."

"Quite," said Signor Ruzzi.

"We've got enough problems with Nutter as it is," added Miss Shepherd.

Nodding and mumbling in the most grovelling way and feeling as low and humble as creatures who lived in the bottom-most black sludge of the deepest, grottiest pond, Tom, Miles and Susan shambled off down a path like a collection of lame worms, looking fearfully all the while for any sign of Orcon or Porcon.

When they got out beyond the lawn, through the woods and into a nearby field, they sat down gloomily. Then Miles said, "We were lucky this time."

95

Tom picked at the dry earth under the grass with the metal point of his laces, feeling very shaken. "But for how long? Porcon will be getting at us all the time now. There's no escape. He can make us do anything."

"If only we could avoid him," said Susan. "Particularly his eyes."

"The only person who might be able to help us is Asquith Minor because he's their friend," said Tom, plucking dismally at some grass. "But after what he's seen, he's such a coward, he's not going to be on our side."

"And can you blame him, really?" said Susan.

"Not really," said Miles. They stared dolefully at each other as the sun sank slowly behind the school.

"Your *brother*?" said Mr Fox, when Orcon took Porcon along to Mr Fox's study the next day to introduce him. He had been getting increasingly concerned about the lack of news from Orcon's parents – and the prospect of educating another boy without any certainty of fees put him into a panic.

"My brother, Porcon, sir," said Orcon. "He's been ill."

"Not with anything infectious, I hope," said Mr Fox, suspiciously, leaning forward on his desk to examine the new arrival. He certainly was Orcon's brother, there was no mistaking it.

"Oh no, sir," said Porcon, reassuringly. "Just a touch of ozonitis. Soon cured with a spot of radiation."

"Radiation?" said Mr Fox. "Don't you mean medication?"

"Yes, yes," said Orcon, hurriedly. "My brother is so clever, sir, he sometimes muddles up the simplest things."

"Clever, eh?" Mr Fox's eyes gleamed. They could do with another genius in the school – for the week Nutter was coming at least. "As clever as you, Orcon?"

"Cleverer," said Orcon. "Brilliant."

Mr Fox paused. He didn't want to appear too keen. "Well, let's say that's satisfactory for the next couple of weeks, shall we? But really, I simply must hear from your parents. I've searched my files and I have no record of your registration. Your parents should have put down a deposit. This is a private school, you know."

"Oh, they'll be in touch, never you fear," said Orcon. "They're just so busy jetting about. I've written to them about the science block, too," he lied. "And they're keen to put a lot of money into it."

Mr Fox perked up. "If I could just have their address?"

Porcon shook his head. "They travel so much, sir," he said. "I had their address last week but now they've moved on again. We're waiting for them to get in touch with us." Orcon gave a smirk that Mr Fox couldn't see.

"Very well," sighed Mr Fox. "But this is an unsatisfactory state of affairs. It can't go on for ever."

And with that he dismissed them. He sighed. Oh, well, even if the parents never showed up, at least Orcon and Porcon would be bound to help the school pass Clive Nutter's rigorous tests. He leant over to the shelf of Lowe's Latin Primers, reached behind and drew out his faithful whisky bottle. He took the inner glass holder from his inkwell and poured a large quantity of whisky into it. He took a huge gulp and then placed the glass with the remaining whisky back into the metal holder and shut the lid for another time. Another time came rather quicker than usual and after ten minutes he'd consumed the lot.

That afternoon, exhausted after dismantling all the sports day equipment and tidying it up singlehanded, Tom, Miles and Susan mooched drearily round the edges of the tennis courts. A few pupils were banging balls at each other over a sagging net; others watched from the sidelines, leaning against the rusty wire netting and scuffing their shoes on the green stones of the court. Susan bounced a bald ball she'd found on the path and when it rolled into the nearby pond none of them could be bothered to try to retrieve it. Tom kicked the gravel as he walked, scuffing up showers of stones ahead of him; Miles punched his head with his fist in time with his steps as if he were trying to hit the memory of what had happened from his mind. Far away the church clock chimed five. They sloped along the path, up past the site where the builders were working on the science block.

"Cheer up, it'll never happen," said Alf, one of the builders, noticing their forlorn faces as they passed. He was bending an enormous piece of metal into a hoop.

"I wouldn't be too sure," said Miles. "Anything could happen in this dump."

"At least you've got birds here," said Bill. "Some posh schools are short of crumpet."

"Crumpet?" said Susan, shocked. "Do you mind not referring to me as something you cook on the end of a fork in front of a roaring fire at Christmas? How would you like me to refer to you as a marshmallow?"

"As long as I could toast you on my fork, you could call me what you liked!" said the third builder, Fred, eyeing Susan lecherously.

Susan couldn't think of anything to say but "Tsk!" and raised her eyebrows at the two boys.

"How's it getting along?" asked Tom, changing the subject. "What's that for?" he added, pointing to the metal. "That's a weird thing for a lab."

"Search me," said Bill. "It looks to me like the car for a Big Wheel in a funfair. There are thirty of them in the plans. All hanging off a huge wheel. I thought this was going to be a place where you learnt how to make atom bombs, not to ride on dodgems! Still, I never did do science at school."

Miles looked astonished. "Can I see the plans?" he said.

"Help yourself," said Alf. "Look, there's one of them water shutes – and there's a whirling drum which makes you stick to the sides. I've told your headmaster but he won't listen. What a berk."

"You can say that again," said Susan, peering over Miles' shoulder. "Look, there's a haunted house – and isn't that a loop-the-loop on a Big Dipper?"

"Great!" said Tom. "But I thought this was a science block?"

"So did we, mate," said the third builder. "But these are the plans we was given and these are the plans we've got to build to. Talking to your headmaster's like talking to a brick wall."

"Of which there don't seem to be a great number at the moment," said Susan, looking around.

"Well, they're not on the plans, are they? They were on the first plans, at least the foundations were, and we've built those, but these new plans are quite different."

Tom suddenly stared at Miles. "It's Orcon again! This is what he and Asquith Minor were designing in

99

the computer room! Look, this page is just like that bit of paper you got when we went in after we'd found Sara carving outside, you remember. We could never work out what it was!"

"You're right!" breathed Miles. "Cripes! A funfair. That'd be brilliant!"

"Until Fox finds out," said Susan, acidly. Her remarks cast rather a pall on the proceedings. "Then what?"

"Nutter will close down the school!" said Miles, grinning. "And we'll all go home! And Mr Fox will be sacked!"

"Correction," said Susan. "Mr Fox will be sacked – and Nutter will take over!"

An appalled silence fell over the three friends.

"Not Nutter!" said Tom.

"My brother went to a school where Nutter taught ages ago – and said he was *horrible*!" said Miles. "Compulsory cold showers, classes segregated into boys and girls, endless punishments, outward bound courses …"

They stared at one another. "We've got to stop those spaceboys," said Miles. "I don't care how we do it. We've just got to risk it. I'd rather be expelled from here than stick around with Nutter as head!"

"Same here!" said Tom.

"Me too," said Susan.

And, saying goodbye to the builders, they walked along the path back to Burlap Hall and tea. But the spring in their steps soon faded. True, they had resolved to do *something*. The only problem was – what?

CHAPTER SEVEN

Days before Nutter's arrival at the school Mr Fox had insisted that every classroom be cleaned out, desks dusted, sheets washed, gym bars polished, tables scrubbed, lawns mown and so on. Holes in the carpet were covered by strategically placed bits of furniture; wobbling banisters were hastily glued into place, chips on white paintwork had been touched up with Tipp-Ex and chips on black paintwork had been touched up with ink. To rid the place of the dismal smell of cabbage and dirty socks, Mr Fox himself had bought five cans of Freshair spray, and now the whole school reeked of Alpine Forest Fragrance ("a carefully blended mixture of alpine herbs, bark and evergreen oils. Also contains Hexatropin 95mg"). A blue rinse was added to all the lavatory cisterns to conceal the brown scummarks engrained in the enamel; whenever anyone peed, the water changed to green. Signor Ruzzi had stayed up the whole night trying to mend a broken note on the piano with bits of felt and fuse-wire and Mr Roy had been detailed to bring back some kind of surface to the green baize of the ancient snooker table by scratching at it vigorously with an old toothbrush.

Every pupil had his or her shoes inspected to see that they were gleaming, backs of necks and knees were checked for grime and hair had to be brushed till it glistened.

Even Mr Fox took his suit in to be cleaned, which was something of a major event. The cleaners took one look and advised strongly against it on the grounds that, held together as it was by layers of dirt, it might fall apart – but Mr Fox thought he'd take the risk.

Finally, the day of Nutter's inspection arrived. Mr Fox decided to harangue the school at assembly, like a coach before an important football match; he'd chosen suitably stirring hymns, and he wore his gown (but more out of necessity than anything else as the cleaners had been right and the trousers of his suit had become so transparent that you could see his kneecaps through them). Before he addressed the school, he coughed ceremoniously.

"Today we are to be inspected. This is a very common procedure to ensure that the school is up to standard. In the case of Burlap Hall, of course, we all know there is no need for it to be examined. Its reputation carries far and wide as one of the centres of academic excellence ..." (here Miles looked at Tom with a quizzical stare) "but it is right that we should be given a chance to reveal our exceptionally high standards to the local authority. The higher our own standards, the higher will be the standards among schools generally. Thus the impression we make on the schools' inspector will not only benefit us but benefit society as a whole – nay, the whole country, if not the whole world."

"'Nay'?" whispered Simon. "Silly ass!" Several of his friends started giggling.

Mr Fox looked at his watch. "The inspector, Mr Clive Nutter, will be arriving in quarter of an hour. I want you to welcome him to the school, to call him 'sir', to make his visit as pleasant as possible and, of course, to show him that our manners are just as impeccable as our education."

There was a great rumbling sound as the pupils shuffled out, all chattering and whispering, slightly dreading the prospect of this strange man sitting in on classes.

The only pupils who didn't seem to be alarmed were Orcon and Porcon. For some reason they were smiling quietly to themselves; and then, with an occasional outburst of hysterical giggling, they'd clutch on to each other, splitting their sides.

"'Make his visit as pleasant as possible!'" howled Orcon, nudging his brother in the ribs – if, that is, he had any ribs to nudge. "'Show him our manners are just as impeccable as our education!'" shrieked Porcon, spluttering with laughter, his fat cheeks reddening and dimpling with merriment. "I can't wait!"

Meanwhile Mr Fox sat in his study, dreading Nutter's arrival and feeling dizzy and sick at the prospect of meeting him again. He stared gloomily out of the window as he heard the sound of Nutter's bicycle crunch on the drive; then, suddenly panicking, he seized the inkwell to devour the remains of his whisky. Unfortunately he'd forgotten that in a fit of tidiness and efficiency he'd actually refilled his inkwell properly and, spitting it out with a furious shout, found his chin and mouth covered with black ink.

Of all things to happen! On today of all days! He rushed to the bathroom and, finding a pumice stone, rubbed at his face until the skin was bright red and raw, stained with black. Bumping into Miss Shepherd in the corridor, he was alarmed by the look of horror that passed over her face when she saw him.

"You drank *ink*!" she said, amazed, when he tried to explain.

"I can't go into it now," said Mr Fox desperately. "Let me borrow some powder from you!" He wrestled with her bag and plunged into it to find some powder – and it was at the moment when he was putting the final touches to his face, staring at the mirror in her compact, that Clive Nutter was ushered up the stairs by a boy consigned to welcome him.

It was not an auspicious start to the day. Nutter looked extremely suspicious as Mr Fox snapped the compact shut and returned it to Miss Shepherd; he instantly got out a notebook and wrote something down in it.

"Welcome, Mr Nutter!" cried Mr Fox, trying desperately to retrieve the situation. "Welcome! Allow me – a cup of coffee in my study before we start! Let me show you our syllabus! I'm certain you'll be favourably impressed."

Nutter reluctantly followed Mr Fox into his study and sat down.

In the sunlight streaming through the study window, Mr Fox saw Clive Nutter more distinctly; a shiver ran through him. There he was, clear as day, just as he remembered him. He had a thin, narrow face the yellowish colour of a hospital ward; his eyes were black pinpricks like pencil-holes in the snow and, carved from the sides of the pitted lump in the middle of his face that passed for a nose down to the sides of the narrow slit in the middle of his face that was, presumably, his mouth, were two deeply-etched lines of bitterness and cruelty. His mousy hair was smarmed tightly to his scalp with a central parting that showed white, greasy skin, and in the middle of his forehead was a twisted line of hatred that gave him a permanent frown. He coughed, disapprovingly.

"Do you always wear make-up, Headmaster?" The inspector's voice was icy as he produced his notebook once again and waited, with pen poised, for Mr Fox's answer.

"Make-up? Good heavens no!" said Mr Fox, trying to laugh. "Just something in my eye, that's all."

"Oh yes?" Clive Nutter didn't look as if he believed a word of it. He scribbled something and stared at his rival. Then he cast his eyes round the room, pen at the ready. "Out-of-date encyclopaedia with two volumes missing," he murmured to himself as he wrote. "Empty inkwell. Unpleasant smell of cigars mixed with toxic air-freshener. Bad example to rest of school." Then, as Mr Fox again suggested coffee, a terrible spasm of pain seemed to cross his face, an expression which Mr Fox presumed, rightly, to be Nutter's attempt at a smile.

"I'll have no coffee, thank you," he said. "Stimulants of any kind are not to be encouraged, particularly when there are children in the proximate vicinity." Mr Fox looked puzzled. He rather wondered what "proximate" meant. Still, it wouldn't look good to ask, so he said nothing and simply offered Nutter a copy of the syllabus.

"I'll study this back at the department in committee with my colleagues," replied Nutter. "But now I would request that the inspection commences. My time is short."

"Oh good," said Mr Fox, involuntarily. Then he shook his head. "I mean, it's good you're so efficient," he added lamely. "No point in wasting time, is there?"

"None at all," said Mr Nutter rising, notebook still in hand and pen at the ready. His beady eyes took everything in before he left the room. "Paint peeling," he whispered to himself as he wrote, "carpet worn. No fire doors." Then, as he stepped outside and looked around again – "Dangerous linoleum; no smoke alarms. Faulty catches on windows. Stair-rods missing on staircarpet. Temperature too high." He stared out of the window as he walked down the corridor, his sick-coloured mackintosh flapping round his greasy, pale-grey trousers. "Dustbins wrongly placed. Unhygienic ..." and on and on like this until he reached the first classroom where Miss Shepherd was teaching the smaller boys and girls.

"I'd prefer to attend this lesson alone," he said, turning to Mr Fox as he entered. "I would get a better feel of the teaching standards without your presence."

"Presents? Surely you don't want any presents from me?" said Mr Fox, startled.

"Presents? Certainly not!" Nutter's face seized up into a different kind of spasm, as if he were drinking vinegar. "Are you accusing me of asking for bribes? Because if you are, I can assure you – "

"No, no," cried Mr Fox, groaning inside. He pushed open the door of the classroom for Nutter to enter, averting his eyes for fear of what he might see. And it was fortunate for him that he didn't look. Because, had he done so, he would have seen a row of young faces all with curiously glazed expressions on their faces. As if they had been hypnotized.

Mr Fox tottered back to his study and waited. He waited and waited. He thought of taking a nip of whisky – but what if Clive Nutter suddenly arrived back and caught him red-handed? He couldn't risk it. He watched the clock on the wall, then looked up at it again after what seemed like ages – but the time still appeared to be the same. It was incredible how slowly time went when you were waiting. After what seemed like another ten minutes, he looked again and seeing the hands *still* in the same position, he consulted his watch. Good heavens! That morning, in an unprecedented move of efficiency, he'd put the clock right and had wound it up, but it was so long since he'd bothered with it he hadn't realized until now that it was broken. No doubt Clive Nutter's eagle eye would spot that as well and he'd write "broken clock" in his notebook.

Finally the bell rang for break.

At a knock on the door he called, "Come in!" hoping to see Clive Nutter there – but it was only Miss Shepherd, looking faint and exhausted.

"Well, how did it go?" hissed Mr Fox. "Where's Nutter?"

Miss Shepherd fell into a chair and passed a trembling hand over her forehead.

"What's happened?" she moaned. "The children seem to have forgotten everything! Everything! When he asked them what two and two was, not one of them could answer. All they said was 'Don't know and don't care.' And – and one of them called him 'twit-face'! Can you imagine it!"

Mr Fox went bright red and his eyes bulged. "They what?" he said, finally. Then, "Well, I suppose they got one thing right. He has got a face like a twit. But what's got into them? What's going on? Where's Nutter?"

"Then, when I was doing craft with the other class, all the children knotted their macramé together and threatened to string Mr Nutter up if he didn't watch it!"

"But where is he now?" said Mr Fox, exasperatedly.

"He insisted on staying behind to write up his notes. He seemed delighted things were going so badly. It was awful. And then he said he'd go down to watch the children play in break." Miss Shepherd put her face into her hands and wept.

Mr Fox leapt up out of his chair and stared out of the window. "Watch them during break! Who's supervising them?"

"Mr Carstairs. Oh, Mr Fox. I'm sorry. I just don't understand what happened!"

But Mr Fox wasn't listening. He was staring out of the window and watching what he saw on the lawn. About forty children were all stampeding round the grass, swearing and cursing, sticking their tongues out at Nutter and Mr Carstairs, pushing each other and shrieking. Then they started chanting together:

"Down with school!
Down with school!
Mr Fox's a drunken fool!
Carstairs's thick,
Mrs Grain's fat,
And Nutter is
AN UTTER PRAT!"

"Oh my God," said Mr Fox. "They've gone completely mad. Fetch Mr Roy. He'll be taking the next class Nutter's inspecting. We must do everything we can to redeem the situation. Though it's probably already too late."

Within minutes Mr Roy was sitting in Mr Fox's study, trying to reassure him.

"Gym's next on the timetable. Nothing can go wrong there. And there'll be no problems in *my* class," he said, smugly. "Look, Orcon and Porcon are bound to give a good impression. And Tom, Miles and Susan and Rosemary – and Sheila, they're all pleasant children. Now don't worry about a thing. Cook has prepared a delicious lunch and Nutter will be in a much better mood this afternoon."

Nothing could go wrong in gym? Lots of things could go wrong in gym – and did. Orcon and Porcon had both scrambled to the top of the bars and stayed there for the whole session, like giant tree-spiders looking down on everyone. As a result they were able to aim their hypnotic gazes on anyone below. One boy found himself leaping higher and higher on the trampoline until, with unerring accuracy, he leapt straight off and on to Nutter's head, felling him to the ground. Another sprang off the vaulting horse into his face; several children found themselves simply unable to get down from the bars when called; they were stuck to the walls like glue until Orcon and Porcon decided to release them. The final indignity was when Nutter, who was standing on an exercise mat at the side of the room, was thrown once again to the ground when three giggling children rushed up to him and pulled the mat from under his feet.

It was an extremely battered and furious Nutter, a Nutter covered with sticking plaster, who partook of lunch with Mr Fox in the dining room.

"I am shocked and horrified," he said as he sat down, waving the soup away. "I am allergic to soup!" he added. "And I don't know why you are giving soup to the children," he added, looking around disapprovingly at the throng of pupils slurping and sucking on their spoons. The dainty cubes of fried bread that Mr Fox had insisted be provided with the soup on this special occasion were not being eaten by anyone; they were being used as ammunition, flicked on the backs of spoons all over the room.

"They should be lunching on cold cuts and boiled potatoes if you ask me. Swedes and turnips are a good source of vitamin C and if you give them ice-cream for pudding," he added, noticing tubs arranged on nearby tables for the last course, "you will be encouraging heart disease, not to mention greed and grossness. No chipped potatoes for me," he said, as the cook tried to tempt him with the main course, "and steak and peas are far too extravagant. No wonder you can't afford a science block. You spend all this money on steaks – and mustard! Mustard! Mustard will only give the children fiery tempers. No wonder they're so badly behaved. And as for gravy – you're spoiling them, Mr Fox!"

The headmaster was about to reply when a water fight broke out at the other end of the table, orchestrated by Orcon and Porcon, and he had to dodge to miss a flying jug that came hurtling his way and broke on the wall behind him.

Clive Nutter looked shocked. "Do you have another notebook I could use, Mr Fox? I'm afraid I have had to write down so many adverse criticisms that I have filled mine already. Unprecedented."

Before Nutter arrived to inspect Mr Roy's class, the geography teacher took the opportunity to try to inspire his pupils. True, the children had behaved appallingly in every other class, but he was determined that his class would be the exception.

"You *must* behave," he said, leaning earnestly over the desk and positively pleading with them. "And for heaven's sake, show some manners and some intelligence! Clive Nutter has been horrified by what he's seen so far at Burlap Hall. It's up to you to rectify the situation. The future of Burlap Hall is in your hands!"

But his earnest enthusiasm was dampened by the sight of Orcon and Porcon sitting at the back, grinning like Cheshire cats.

"I suppose we'd better pull the stops out," whispered Tom to Miles. "Goes against the grain – but we don't want Nutter as head."

Miles nodded. "But it's easier said than done," he said, dejectedly. "I wish I could get out of Porcon's line of vision."

At that moment Nutter came in and sat down in front of the class. He pursed the two worms on his face that passed for lips, sniffed suspiciously through his pickle-like nose and waited.

"Ah, now, geography," said Mr Roy, smiling encouragingly at the class. "I'd like you, Susan, to explain how rocks are formed."

Susan started. "Rocks are formed by sediment …" but as she spoke she felt a burning in the back of her head. She tried to keep her mouth shut as she felt a string of awful words about to leap out, but she couldn't.

"Sediment," she continued.

"Yes?" asked Mr Roy, smiling, trying not to belie the desperation he felt inside.

"Just that," snapped Susan. "Sediment. OK? So what's it to you how rocks are formed? I'll thank you not to ask personal questions. I'll keep what I know about rocks to myself, you big busybody. How dare you pry into my private life! What I know about how rocks are formed is no one's business but my own!"

There was a gasp of horror from the class and Susan clapped a hand over her mouth.

"Perhaps you'd go on, Miles," said Mr Roy, starting

to panic. "Rocks."

Miles stared. Every scrap of information he possessed about rocks had vanished from his mind. He scraped round each nook and cranny of his brain and came up with – nothing at all.

"Rocks?" he said. "What are they?"

"Tom!" said Mr Roy, now desperate. "Please tell us everything you know about rock formation."

Tom stared at Mr Roy. He knew that Porcon at that very moment was staring at him. He did his best to resist but he couldn't. He clamped his mouth tight shut but he could feel his tongue pressing hard against his lips. Out it popped and waggled derisively at Mr Roy. Worse still, he felt his hands moving to grasp his geography book and slowly lift it – before throwing the book straight at the geography master. Finally, although he tried desperately to control himself, he felt his hands forcing their way up to each side of his face; then one thumb of each hand sprang out, jammed itself into each of his ears and his fingers wiggled scornfully at Mr Nutter.

"Rocks?" he heard himself saying, or rather yelling. "You can stick 'em up your jumper for all I care!"

The class was in pandemonium. Frantically, Mr Roy tried to call on Orcon or Porcon to speak – but Clive Nutter could take no more. He rose from his chair, turned to Mr Roy and, with a ghastly grimace, said, "Thank you very much for letting me attend your class. It has been most illuminating." And then he left the room, leaving Susan in tears, Miles and Tom turning furiously on Porcon, and Mr Roy with his head in his hands as the rest of the class just looked on, astonished.

*　　*　　*

Orcon and Porcon didn't stay to hear what Mr Roy had to say to them. They rushed from the room shrieking with laughter, followed rather half-heartedly by Asquith Minor whose smile seemed a little forced; then they all ran down the corridor to Mr Fox's study. The door had just closed with a furious bang as Clive Nutter demanded an audience with the headmaster. The three pressed their ears to the door and listened.

"An outrage!" Clive Nutter was saying. "A complete outrage!"

"But wait – wait till you've seen our sports at least!" Mr Fox was pleading. "This afternoon's cricket match, for example, is a splendid …"

"There's no time for that! The sooner I return to my office to start putting wheels into motion, the better!" replied Nutter, furiously. "This school should be closed down at once! On the spot! Your resignation will be demanded as soon as possible!"

At the mention of resignation, Mr Fox finally flipped.

"How dare you!" he yelled. "You can't demand my resignation, you jumped-up little schools' inspector. It needs the board of governors' consent to get me to resign!"

"Board of governors! A fig for the board of governors!" said Clive Nutter. "I shall go straight back to my superior at the Town Hall and I shall bring him here next week to see for himself what a shambles you are running in the name of education. Once he has signed the necessary forms, the rest is mere formality. I would not be at all surprised if you weren't thrown out. Out! Out!"

"Out?" said Mr Fox, appalled. "But who would run the school?"

Clive Nutter sounded smug and satisfied as he spoke. "As you know, it has always been my ambition to be the headmaster of Burlap Hall. I shall apply for the job and when I get it this place will be completely restructured.

"For a start, all the teachers will be sacked. I have a few colleagues who know how to teach, unlike the sad specimens you call staff, and they will be brought in before the end of term. I shall insist that all pupils rise at 5.30 a.m. for a cold shower, followed by a compulsory run twenty times round the grounds in their shorts, whatever the weather. Girls and boys will be strictly segregated and have classes on their own.

"I will introduce boxing as a form of sport at the school to toughen the boys up – and, of course, the girls as well – and outward-bound courses will be compulsory. No half-terms will be allowed and Saturdays will be included as a working day, with Sundays to be spent entirely in church except for an hour's relaxation when the children can study their bibles and write letters home. Letters which, of course, will be censored by myself. Television will be banned, also radios and novels. Fagging will be re-introduced – I can't think why you ever got rid of that system – and lights out will be at 7.00 p.m. Any boy or girl who disobeys the rules will be severely beaten – and as for the uniform it will have to be completely re-designed. Shorts for all ages and all seasons, preferably in bright purple and orange to make the pupils easily spotted. And stout boots and boaters. Haircuts will be compulsory once a week – by the school barber. Understand?"

There was a low moan from the study, presumably from Mr Fox.

"You can't do this to me!" he was saying. "I've tried

so hard to make this a happy school, a school of high academic achievement, of creativity ..."

"Happy?" snapped Clive Nutter. "Happy? Schools are not meant to be happy! They are meant to form strong characters and good citizens. Happiness is a red herring!"

Orcon and Porcon prised their ears from the door and put their gloved hands over their mouths. They could hardly stifle their laughter.

"I wish we could stay to see this!" said Orcon. "I'd love to see you all on your early morning runs!"

Asquith Minor looked surprised. "Stay? Why, are you going?"

Porcon sneered. "You don't think we'd stick around for that kind of regime, do you? This has been the funniest few weeks of my life! Hard luck, Asquith Minor!"

"But where will you go?" Asquith Minor suddenly felt even more worried than he had done before. However strange, they were his friends. And now they were betraying him. They were landing the whole school in the soup and then going off.

"We'll go home!" laughed Orcon. "Ha ha ha ha!"

There was something about that laugh that made Asquith Minor's blood run cold.

"But we're friends!" he protested. "You can't leave me here on my own ..."

"Can't we?" Porcon sneered at him. "You just wait!"

Asquith Minor was outraged. After all he'd done for them. He'd protected Orcon when he'd arrived, he'd helped them understand how the school worked and explained things to them. And now they were going and leaving him to cope with the Nutter regime all by himself. He felt moved to make a protest.

"You're going nowhere!" he said, sharply. "I'm going straight in there and telling Mr Fox exactly what you've been up to! I'm going to tell him that it's you who are responsible for all this! Then he'll expel you and we can get back to normal."

As soon as he'd said it, he rather wished he hadn't. Orcon's big eyes suffused with anger and Porcon's fat cheeks wobbled indignantly. "Just you try!" said Orcon. "I don't think you'll get very far! You know what we can do, don't you! You might well find yourself saying something else! Anyway," he added sulkily, "you were just as keen on the funfair as me."

"Yes, you'll have a great time with that in the grounds," interrupted Porcon. "It won't be all bad."

"You don't think Nutter will allow a funfair to be built, do you?" said Asquith Minor. "Mr Fox may be a chump, but Nutter would spot a dodgem car a mile off."

"We'll just have time, I think," said Orcon, looking at his watch, "for the funfair to be built, and to have a really good time on it, before Nutter comes and then we'll go home. It'll be brill!"

Asquith Minor paused and thought. He couldn't let them get away with it. He tried again. "I'll tell Mr Fox when you're not around," he said, threateningly. He felt all hot and red. "You can't be with me all the time."

Porcon suddenly looked a lot less friendly. He gripped Asquith Minor by the arm. "You do that and you know what we'll do?"

Asquith Minor struggled vainly. "Let go!" he yelled.

"We'll send you to our neighbouring planet. The planet Or. It's next to ours, the planet Er. And you

116

won't like that, I can tell you!"

"Planet?" said Asquith Minor. "What do you mean, planet? You mean Tom and Miles were right! You *are* from outer space!"

"Of course," said Orcon. "How do you think we get our powers? It's not magic, you know."

Asquith Minor felt like crying. He must be dreaming, having a nightmare after watching a horror film. He'd soon wake up. It couldn't be true. And yet the tight grip on his arm was painfully real.

"Yes, Porcon," said Orcon, "I think Or would be a great place for Asquith Minor. He'd like the environment. Of course with his feet it would be difficult wouldn't it, on the water. He couldn't paddle, like us, could he?"

"Paddle?"

"Paddle!" said Orcon.

Prompted by the idea of this peculiar activity, Asquith Minor took a longer, harder look at the two "boys". They'd always looked a *bit* odd, but suddenly he saw them in a completely different light. They didn't look human, really. Their heads were far too big; their necks too thin; their hair too wispy. Their eyes were too big to be natural and then there was that greenish tinge to their faces – a colour which seemed to be increasing in depth of tone every moment he looked at them.

To his horror, Orcon was moving. He was slowly pulling at one of his gloves. Asquith Minor could hardly bear to look. Then Orcon gave a great tug and pulled off the glove completely – to reveal a dreadful sight. For underneath was not a hand! Instead Orcon had a scaly, webbed paw, like a duck's foot covered with fish's scales, but with the added horror of long hard brown claws at the end of five horny green finger-like protuberances. "Paddle! You need these to paddle," he said.

Porcon was looking at his brother's hand with interest. "Good heavens," he said, seizing it, "your claws are even longer than mine and I'm older than you. When *will* Dad clip our claws, do you think? I just can't stand this much longer. *Everyone* in my class in Er has their claws clipped. It's just not fair."

Orcon shrugged. "He's got to do it sometime soon. He can't keep us as young kids for ever."

Porcon nodded, and then turned his attention back to Asquith Minor who was looking extremely queasy.

"And he might not like the food," said Porcon, referring to Asquith Minor with a mocking laugh. Orcon leant against the wall with a mean grin on his moon-like face. "No! We don't have the muck you call food up there. We just have metal. And then only sometimes!"

"On Er things are quite different."

"But he wouldn't be going to Er, would he?" said Orcon, laughing. "He'd be going to Or!"

Asquith went as white a sheet. "You – you – " and then he stopped. Because Asquith Minor was not so dumb as to fail to realize that, at this moment, survival was the most important thing in his life. If he didn't go along with them, who knew what they might do to him? They might take him back with them and chop his head off and mount it on a piece of wood; they might use him as a slave; they might exhibit him in a space freak-show. This was no time to be brave. It was a time to be cunning.

He tried his best to relax. "Only kidding," he said nonchalantly. "Forget it." But inside himself he was thinking that he must get to Tom, Miles and Susan as soon as possible. Only with their help might these two monstrous creatures be persuaded to return to their own planet.

At that moment the door of Mr Fox's study burst open and Clive Nutter marched out, his eyes glittering victoriously.

"See you again very soon, Mr Fox," he said, in a voice like ice. "And if I were you I'd start taking the *Times Educational Supplement* and look in the Employment column. You could find there's a vacancy as a caretaker at a state primary school. You never know, you *might* get a job like that. *If* you're lucky!"

CHAPTER EIGHT

"Where's my sock!" Miles was yelling, hopping about on one leg on the wooden floor of the games hut. He and Tom were getting ready for the second cricket match against St Beowulf's.

"If you walk very slowly no one will notice you've got one black sock," said Tom, who was tying on his pads.

"But the whole point of cricket is to run fast!" moaned Miles. "I can't catch a ball walking slowly."

"Oh, who cares?" said Tom. "It's the stupidest game in the world. I wish I was scoring. Then at least I wouldn't have to dress up in these ridiculous clothes. Honestly! Look at me," he said to Miles as he got up and lumbered around in pads six sizes too big. His mother had told him he'd grow into them and they practically came up to his nose. "I look like a Martian."

It was at this point that Asquith Minor rushed up, red in the face from running. He was late. "That's what they are!" he said, gasping. "You're right! Only they don't come from Mars, they come from Er. Or Or."

Miles turned to him scornfully. "Oh shut up," he said. "You're talking rubbish."

But Tom turned to Asquith Minor. "What did you say? Do you mean Orcon and Porcon?"

"Yes," gasped Asquith Minor. "They're from outer space. They showed me their hands – I mean their – " he couldn't describe them in a single word – "their beastly webbed things covered with scales with great long claws at the end. It was horrible. And they said they'd send me to Or – or Er – if I told!"

Miles sighed. "Can't you speak properly?" he said. "What's all this or or, er er, or or stuff?"

"It's the name of their planet," said Asquith Minor desperately. "Er. With a capital O. Er, I mean, E. No, that's where they're going to send me to. No, sorry, it was Or. Or was it Er. It was either Er or Or."

"I've never heard of planets called Er or Or," said Tom.

"Oh God, now you're at it," said Miles. "Will no one find my sock? I can't stand it!"

"Nor can I," said Asquith Minor.

"Not Nor as well as Or and Er," sighed Miles. "This is too much." He started rummaging about in a cupboard until a box fell off a shelf, spilling croquet balls all over the floor. Sighing, Miles picked them up and stuffed them back.

"I mean I haven't heard of them, either," said Asquith Minor. "But I guess in outer space they have different names for their planets. It's hardly likely that they call them Venus and Uranus and so on. They probably call Earth something like Cor."

"Cor?" said Miles. "Blimey!"

"Stop it!" said Tom to Miles. "Can't you see? He believes us! He's found out more about them. Come on – tell!"

As Asquith Minor gasped out his story, not forgetting the bit about Clive Nutter, Miles calmed down. He forgot about his sock and stared at Asquith Minor.

"So they've admitted it!" he said. "But what are we going to do?"

"You're friends with them," said Tom. "Look, keep it that way. Don't let on you've talked to us. Try and find out more about their planet. Where it is. Anything.

If we know where they live maybe we can get them back up there." He didn't sound very hopeful but it was all he could think of. Asquith Minor nodded, sat down on a bench and started to change into his whites. He pulled his cricket clothes out of his bag. "Hang on," he said, holding up something small and white, "I've got three socks. Does this one belong to anyone?"

It was easier said than done. Now Asquith Minor knew their real story, Orcon and Porcon were on their guard. When he asked them where Er and Or were they would only reply, mysteriously, "Wouldn't you like to know!" And when he protested that he knew they came from outer space and asked what harm it could be just knowing where the planets were, they looked mysterious.

"Up there," said Orcon, pointing vaguely to the sky. "No, down there," said Porcon, pointing with a gloved hand. "Remember it's summer here and the sun is now to the west, so if you include the angle of sixty-five degrees and take into account the earth's stratosphere, we must be above Australia."

"Or there again, we might not. It all depends on what you call Venus is up to at the moment."

"Ah, yes," smiled Porcon, enigmatically, folding his arms smugly over his fat tummy. "The year of the eclipse."

None of this made any sense to Asquith Minor.

He racked his brains as to how he might find out more. He searched their lockers when they were in class; he raided their desks at night. He looked in their games kits, he peered under their beds and he rifled through their coat pockets. All he could find, written on a piece of computer paper which was stuffed into a pocket of Orcon's computer folder, were the words Or and Er. He thought it was nothing to start with. But, as he realized that it was the only scrap of evidence he could find to substantiate the fact they were from outer space, he told Tom, Miles and Susan about it.

They all met the following afternoon in Miles and Tom's room. They were meant to be writing letters to their parents, but this was an emergency. Their parents would have to wait for a week.

"Perhaps we could pull their gloves off and show Mr Fox?" suggested Miles.

"How could we? The minute we attacked them Porcon would hypnotize us. We'd never get so far as revealing a little finger." Tom felt utterly defeated.

"And we couldn't force them to undress, to show they've got no belly buttons, could we?" said Susan.

"No – and anyway, they're the star pupils. None of the teachers *want* to believe there's anything funny about them," said Tom.

"Evidence. Evidence," murmured Susan, twiddling her red hair. She was sitting cross-legged in the corner. "So, we've really got nothing at all – except the scrap of paper that Asquith Minor found."

"Where did you say you found it?" asked Miles.

"In Orcon's computer folder," said Asquith Minor, who was lying on Tom's bed, eating crisps. "But that doesn't mean anything."

"Hang on!" said Tom, struck by an idea. "Maybe it *does* mean something! Perhaps it's their password!"

"What do you mean, password?" asked Asquith Minor, mid-crunch.

"Password. Computer password," said Susan, excitedly. "You know how people sometimes make special programs and protect them with a code-word so no one else can look. You know Orcon and Porcon are always in the computer room – I bet they've got a program to get themselves back to Er or Or and it's stored there, in one of the computers."

Tom jumped up. "Well, let's go and have a look!" he said. Then he stopped, feeling rather wretched. "But I can still hardly work out how to turn the wretched thing on. Hey – you're good at computers," he said to Asquith Minor. "You can help us!"

"I'm only any good when Orcon and Porcon are helping me," said Asquith Minor, reluctantly. "But I'll have a go."

Luckily no one was using the computer room. The Apples were blank; four unfriendly, dead screens.

"Which one?" said Tom, feeling helpless but trying to sound more positive.

"Who knows?" said Asquith Minor, sitting in front of one of them. "Let's take one each and try different passwords."

He switched his on and started. "First we've got to get into the program part. We've got to use the reverse of this disc, that's all I know, and follow the A prompt."

Gradually, between them, they worked out how to get into the part of the computer that held the key to the programs that might have been devised by Orcon and Porcon.

"Here we are!" said Asquith Minor, excitedly, as the screen finally accepted their instructions and flashed up 'Please insert code-word. A>'. "Look, it's asking for our password! If we can put in the right password, then we might get their special program!"

First they all tried the password "OR". The computer just came up with its usual "?". Then they tried "ER". No luck either. Then "OR AND ER" and then "ER AND OR" but still nothing happened.

"A wild-goose chase," said Miles, gloomily, about to turn his computer off. But Asquith Minor stopped him. "Hang on," he said. "Let me think again. I'm sure the answer's here somewhere." Then he said, "Wait a minute! I think on the piece of paper I found, it said 'OR and ER full-stop'."

"What difference would 'full-stop' make?" asked Susan. "What do you mean?"

"Computers don't recognize as passwords anything except the password reproduced exactly," said Asquith Minor. "So if your password is – I don't know, say 'Susan' in inverted commas, it won't recognize Susan without inverted commas. So that full stop could make all the difference. Let's see ..." He tried "OR AND ER." and "ER AND OR." Then he tried "EROR" then "ORER" then "EROR." and "ORER." He shook his head. "You have a go," he said to the others. "It's worth trying everything. You never know."

Miles tried all the different combinations, then Susan and finally Tom. He felt most depressed about the whole thing. It was such a long shot. It couldn't work. He tried the very last one, "ORER.", and the screen just buzzed.

"No good," he said. He reached for the Off button but Asquith Minor, who'd got up to look at his screen, stopped him. "Hang on – if it won't accept it, it usually comes up with a question mark quicker than this. Maybe this is it."

They all crowded round the screen. The computer continued to buzz fitfully. "I bet this is it," said

Asquith Minor. "You can hear it thinking!"

Finally the computer gave a last buzz and on to the screen sprang a glittering array of green figures and marks, completely incomprehensible to any of them – but something all the same.

"This is it!" said Asquith Minor, punching the air in his excitement. "Whatever it is, it's it! Brilliant! We've done it!"

Although the others were puzzled, Asquith Minor's enthusiasm was catching.

"Quick, print it out! We'll never remember it!" said Tom. "And if they find out we've got into their program they may change it."

"Good idea!" said Asquith Minor. "But how?"

Susan wrestled with a drawer and found a big book of instructions. She looked up Printing. Slowly they worked out how to do it – they turned the printer on and, like magic, it rattled out a piece of paper covered with mysterious signs. The sound was deafening, like bullet-shots from a machine gun. Everyone glanced nervously at the door; finally the printer came to a halt. Tom folded up the paper, put it in his pocket and switched off the computer.

"Now what?" he said.

Asquith Minor was just about to answer. But at that very moment, the door opened – and there stood Orcon and Porcon. They looked weirder than ever, their gloves creepier and woollier than before, as if they'd been fluffed up after a good wash. Knowing that underneath the gloves were scaly hands and fins, Tom found them even more terrifying – and there was something about their thinning hair that gave them the look of people just escaped from a nuclear explosion. They did *not* look healthy.

"Ha!" said Orcon, pointing at them. "And what have you been up to?"

Porcon waddled forward. "Get out," he said. "*We* want to use the computers. Clear off!" He sat down at the computer Asquith Minor had been working at – and a piece of paper beside it caught his eye. "What's this?" he said. "Er? Or? Er and Or? Or and Er?" A sinister look passed over his face as realization dawned. He turned in his chair.

"You've been trying to hack into our program, haven't you?" he said, nastily.

"No we haven't," said Susan. But Tom was thinking faster. He knew Asquith Minor hadn't written down his final ideas, so he tried bluffing.

"Yes, we have," he said. "We tried them all – all the ones on that bit of paper – but none of them worked. So we've given up."

"Ha!" said Orcon. "We got here just in time, then. Change the password, Porcon. At once."

Porcon, rattled away at the machine. "They might have found it if they'd gone on trying," he said. His gloves held up his progress on the keyboard and, with a grunt of anger, he said, "I'm fed up with these gloves. These kids know where we're from. I might as well take them off!" and he gave the fingers a tug with his teeth.

The children recoiled in horror. Because, instead of hands, Porcon had webbed membranes, covered in hard green and brown scales. At the end of each "finger" was a long, pointed, claw-like nail that curved slightly at the tip.

"Ugh!" said Susan, involuntarily.

"What do you, mean 'ugh'?" snapped Porcon. "What do you think we feel like when we see those horrible bald sausages you call fingers? And all attached to that lump of pale flesh you call your palms? Disgusting! Sometimes I want to be sick!"

"And your belly buttons! How can you live with them?" said Orcon, shuddering. "I couldn't bear to have a hole in my tummy."

"They're not holes, they're blind alleys," said Miles, unable to resist explaining anything medical. "They don't lead anywhere."

Porcon put his hands over his ears. "Don't tell us any more. It gives us the creeps." Then he turned to his brother. "What new password shall I use, Orcon?"

"I can't tell you in front of them, you fool," said Orcon. "Look, I'll do the password and you deal with them. I think they should be punished for trying to catch us out, don't you?"

"I do indeed," said Porcon. "Good idea." He rose from his chair staring at the four friends hypnotically. Tom managed to close his eyes quickly and fumbled for the door, but it had mysteriously locked itself. "Open your eyes, Tom," said Porcon, in his thin, reedy voice. "And look at me."

Despite himself, Tom found his eyes slowly opening – and staring straight into Porcon's. He was transfixed. Slowly, they all felt themselves being propelled towards the door. Now it had mysteriously unlocked itself. Outside in the corridor Porcon closed the door behind him.

"And now," he said, rubbing his scaly paws together in gleeful anticipation, "your punishment."

Try as they might to turn their heads away, the four friends could not resist his power. Tom heard his neck creak as, in vain, he attempted to twist his head from the spaceboy's gaze. He tried to keep his eyes shut, but

128

his eyelids were forced up, as if someone were tugging at them with tweezers. There was nothing he could do. He had to give in. Porcon's eyes grew large and dreamy – and then, slowly growing from the centre, emerged the dreaded laser beams, hissing as they grew longer and longer, penetrating each of the children's eyeballs.

"Now let me think. It must be something special this time," said Porcon, with a horrid grin. "Ah, yes. Now, concentrate."

It seemed hours before the laser beams retracted – and the children were left feeling exhausted and dead. They were powerless against his orders. Heaven knows what they'd been made to do, but within seconds their legs seemed to pull them in the direction of Mr Fox's study, giving them a slow, sluggish but, in the end, monotonously relentless step. They walked silently. No one would even have noticed them – except Mr Carstairs whose study door was ajar.

He had just finished reading and re-reading the letter from DATA! DATA! magazine. He'd entered Orcon and Porcon as the Burlap Hall group for the Bits, Bytes, Bauds and Pixcels competition and to his immense delight they'd been shortlisted for the first prize along with only two other groups from neighbouring schools, St. Beowulf's and Hamister House. He was certain Orcon and Porcon would excel at the award ceremony. It was amazing really. He'd only been filling in that term because Mr Fritz, the science teacher, was away ill – and here he was, producing geniuses. Reluctantly he snapped himself out of fantasies of receiving the Nobel Prize and had just picked up a book called *Youth and the Drugs Culture* by Professor Greystraight, when the children had passed his open door. He stared at them and then at the book where he read: "And how can a teacher spot the symptoms of children on drugs? They are invariably sluggish in movement, they seem mesmerized by the toxic substance they have consumed, they are pale and silent and yet their eyes glitter with unknown purpose." That described the kids he'd just seen to a T. He read on, anxiously.

Mr Fox was at that very moment re-reading the letter he had received from Clive Nutter. He had got it that morning but after he'd skimmed through it once he couldn't face looking at it again until he'd had several strong drinks.

"Dear Fox," it started. That was a bad sign. It showed a patronising intimacy that Mr Fox could well do without. "As you know I was extremely disappointed in the standards of manners, education, cleanliness, food, decoration, discipline ..." Mr Fox's eyes whizzed over the next few lines until he got to "... and general management of Burlap Hall.

"I have to tell you that I have recommended a complete re-structuring with regard to the above school, which would, of course, involve your relinquishing your post and a new headmaster being appointed.

"I shall be making another visit with my superior, Bill Babbage, for confirmation of the above suggestions. Once he has countersigned my recommendations, I shall suggest that you resign rather than place yourself in the embarrassing position of being dismissed by the local authority. With every good wish, Clive Nutter."

With every good wish! The gall of that man! How could he write a sentence like that without being choked to death by his conscience? It was preposterous.

He scratched his head before taking another sip from his inkwell. There was no question about it; had Clive Nutter come last term this would never have happened. True, the pupils at Burlap Hall were not all budding Einsteins, but they were good enough and friendly enough and intelligent enough and polite enough to pass any inspection. There must be some reason for this outbreak of unruly behaviour! If only he could find out who were the ringleaders, he could expel them and get back to normal. He took another swig from his inkwell, pushed back his chair, put his legs on his desk and sighed, deeply.

At that very moment he heard the sound of a cheerful song coming from the corridor. It got louder until it stopped outside his own door. There was a sharp knock – and in marched Tom, Miles, Susan and Asquith Minor, all staring straight ahead like zombies.

"What do you want?" barked Mr Fox. "I'm extremely busy! I have no time at the moment. Come back tomorrow!"

Miles stepped forward and bowed. "Please, sir," he said. "Listen to our song. We have written it specially for you, in your honour."

Mr Fox sighed. A song was the last thing he wanted. "Very well," he said. "But make it snappy."

Tom, Miles, Susan and Asquith Minor took their places on the carpet. Miles cleared his throat and then they all carefully put their hands on their hips and opened their mouths. Susan clapped time and Asquith Minor said, "With a *one! two! three! four!*"

And then they sang:

"Oh, *you've* got a cheek,
And *I've* got a cheek,
What cheeky chums are we.
We love to show our rudies,
While chanting: 'Hee hee hee!'
So join us in our chorus,
We think you will agree – that
You've got a cheek
And *I've* got a cheek,
What cheeky chums are we!"

At the final chorus all four of them turned around and Miles, Tom, Susan and Asquith Minor waggled their bottoms at Mr Fox.

Then they swivelled back again and started repeating the verse.

"Stop it!" roared Mr Fox. "Stop it at once!"

But however hard he yelled, they continued, winking and nudging each other through the verses. Finally, the headmaster leapt from his seat and rushed round to the front of his desk. The next time they waggled their bottoms at him he gave them each a hearty slap.

"STOP" (slap!) "IT" (slap!) "AT" (slap!) "ONCE!" (slap!), he roared.

Shocked into consciousness, the children immediately stopped what they were doing and looked at each other in dismay. There was nowhere they could turn without being confronted by a suffocating blanket of shame, shame that didn't just rise from inside themselves but which seemed to force against them from outside as well. It was as if they had been positively marinated in humiliation, humiliation which soaked into every cell of their bodies, every fibre of their clothes.

132

"We're very sorry," squeaked Tom huskily, trying to struggle back to normality.

Asquith Minor was equally repentant, clutching at Mr Fox's coat and practically crying. "I'm sorry, I'm sorry, we didn't mean it!"

"We couldn't help it," said Miles, clasping his hands in front of him as if praying for mercy.

Susan was beetroot red. "I'm sorry," she whispered, faintly.

"Sorry?" said Mr Fox. "Sorry!" Then he sat down at his desk. "SORRY!" he shouted again. "I'll give you sorry! You're expelled!"

"But sir," said Miles, horrified. "We couldn't help it!"

"We were hypnotized by Orcon and Porcon!" said Tom.

"They're from outer space!" said Asquith Minor.

"And they've changed the science block plans into plans for a funfair!" said Miles.

Mr Fox's face slowly turned more and more purple. So these were the children responsible for the disruptive element that had been infecting the school! He had found them out at last.

"EXPELLED!" he yelled. "You've ruined Burlap Hall with your antics! You've lost me my job! You're EXPELLED! I'll write to your parents today and they'll pick you up as soon as possible and take you away! For ever and ever! I never want to see you ever again!"

The four friends stood rooted to the spot. Then Mr Fox, with a howl of rage, leapt up from his seat and, repeating "NEVER AGAIN!" over and over at the top of his voice, shooed them out and slammed the door.

They all stood outside, shaking and staring at each other with white faces.

"Expelled!" said Asquith Minor, horrified. "My dad'll never forgive me!"

"Nor will mine," said Miles.

Susan was trembling. "I never thought I'd find myself doing anything like that! It was – it was *disgusting*! No wonder we're expelled. I'd expel myself if I could." They all stood silently, paralysed with embarrassment. Feelings of complete helplessness and fear surged inside them. Susan started to cry.

Tom put his arm round her, comfortingly. "Cheer up," he said, trying to help. "We can't put the clock back. We mustn't waste time agonizing over it. What can we *do*? That's the problem. Look," he said, trying to be constructive and pulling the printout from his pocket, "I've got that piece of paper. That must mean something, surely."

The others crowded round staring at it, eager to take their minds off the appalling scene they'd just enacted.

"The only person who could make head or tail of this would be Mr Carstairs," said Asquith Minor. "We can't ask him!"

"Why not?" said Susan. "Who else can we ask? And, anyway, now we've got nothing to lose."

Mr Carstairs was still in his study. He had got deeper into his book, while listening to Bros on his record player in an effort to steep himself in the culture of young people and make him empathize even more with the youth of today. On his lap he had a piece of paper on which he was making notes. "Score" he had written. "Scag, heroin, horse, Mary Jane, freebasing(?), Crank." This last was crossed out and "Crack" substituted. The list continued. "Ecstasy, STREET-WISE, STREET-SMART" and so on.

"Hey! Cool!" he said as they came in. "Just reading this great, brill book! I hope you never want to *do drugs*, by the way, as you young people call it. Beware the horse, eh? Scag is a scam!" As he said this, Mr Carstairs looked intently at the four friends. Yes, they seemed to show all the symptoms. Their eyes were bright and glittering, their complexions were white and their bodies shook, generally. It pointed to only one thing.

Tom looked baffled. "Sorry, sir?" he said. "I don't think we know anything about racing."

"Horse! H!" said Mr Carstairs, tapping his nose, knowingly. "You know – heroin. Surely you're always being offered it at the school gates? It says here …"

Miles looked worried. "Heroin? Drugs?" he said. "No one's ever offered it to me. And what's all this about horses, anyway?"

"Whatever you do," said Mr Carstairs, "just remember, you *can't handle it!* I think we understand each other."

Susan interrupted. "Look, sir, some of us have tougher things to worry about than drugs." She sounded prim. "Honestly, adults! They go on about it all the time, don't they?"

"And all the time they're smoking and drinking," said Miles, disapprovingly. "Ridiculous."

"We've been expelled," said Tom, trying to get the conversation back on the right track.

Mr Carstairs looked puzzled. "Expelled? Surely not. First I've heard of it."

"We have," said Asquith Minor. "We've been expelled by Mr Fox. For bad behaviour."

"Well, you have been behaving pretty, er, un-defly, recently," admitted Mr Carstairs.

135

Susan looked baffled. "Look, sir," she said. "Could you try to forget the youth culture? Just talk normally, OK?"

"OK. Right on. Brill. Def. I mean, fine," said Mr Carstairs, confused.

Then Tom explained everything to him, right from the beginning – but the English teacher refused to be convinced.

"Outer space! Come on! Pull the other one!" he said, finally. And yet, at the back of his eyes there lingered a spark of doubt.

"Their gloves – you'll admit they're odd?" said Tom. "And look outside. Surely that's a funfair being built, not a science block?"

"Nonsense!" said Carstairs, getting up and going over to the window to look out. And yet ... And yet ... He'd never seen a science laboratory that featured a rail-track with little cars on it. And that great metal sheet that was slowly being hammered out – it looked remarkably like a Big Wheel, it was true. And surely that weird construction being erected at the back, with its tracks and dips and swerves – it couldn't be anything but the structure for a Big Dipper, there was no getting round it.

On the other hand, it was completely impossible.

"I agree, it's odd," he admitted. "And there does seem to be a lot of circumstantial evidence. But I'm afraid you're living in a dream world." The mention of the words "dream world" reminded him of the professor's book. "Are you *sure* no one's been offering you any horse at the gates? Or any weird substances? Like snow or Mary Jane? You haven't been – er," he quickly consulted his book, "um, chasing the dragon, by any chance?"

Miles started to lose his temper. "Dragons? For goodness sake, sir," he said, exasperatedly. "Oh," he added, noticing the book's title, *Youth and the Drug Culture*. That old stuff."

Tom rummaged in his pocket and handed Mr Carstairs the piece of paper with Orcon and Porcon's secret program on it. "Look – will this convince you?" he said.

Mr Carstairs gave it a cursory glance, pushed it away and shook his head. "What I can't understand is why, if Orcon and Porcon are to blame for all this trouble, Mr Fox hasn't expelled them, not you."

"But he doesn't know it's their fault!" said Asquith Minor, excitedly. "And even if he did know, he couldn't expel them because he doesn't know where their parents live! Because they're from outer space!"

Mr Carstairs scratched his head. "He must know their address," he said. "He knows everyone's addresses. He's got to send the parents the bills. And anyway he'll be inviting Orcon and Porcon's parents to see the final challenge of the Bits, Bytes, Bauds and Pixcels Awards at Lanchester. You know Orcon and Porcon have nearly won that prize? Beaten some of the biggest computer brains in the country. It's a magnificent achievement. But sadly not sufficient, it seems, to impress Clive Nutter."

"They *would* be able to win that, wouldn't they? Doesn't it strike you as strange they've won?" interrupted Susan.

"No offence, sir. I mean you teach computer studies marvellously," added Asquith Minor in an oily way.

"In fact," said Tom, pushing the piece of computer paper towards Mr Carstairs, "we knew that only you could possibly understand this because – because you're so *brilliant* at computer studies!"

He nearly choked as he said it, but it worked because Mr Carstairs was flattered into taking a second look at the computer sheet, this time giving it his full attention. He started to frown. Then he looked again. And again. And he looked harder. And harder. And at every glance he got more and more fascinated. His nose practically touched the paper. Then he reached for his glasses and read the paper far away.

"Good grief!" he said, finally.

"What is it, sir?" asked Asquith Minor.

"This is amazing!" He waved the paper around enthusiastically. "Where did you say you found this? In the computer? Orcon and Porcon's secret file? Well, you certainly couldn't have invented this, that's for sure!"

"What is it?" asked Tom, walking round to the back of the teacher's chair and looking over his shoulder.

"It's – it's, as far as I can make out, something to do with transcending time. A kind of travelling code to transport people from time and space – through a microchip! It's incredible! I've never seen anything like it before!"

"Couldn't we send them back, then?" said Miles. "Using this?"

"Not without their permission, I don't think. I mean, they'd have to have someone helping them the other end. Or they'd have to key it in themselves, as far as I can see. It's all extremely difficult," he said. He shook his head and sighed. Maybe he wasn't in line for the Nobel prize after all.

"So you do believe us, sir?" said Susan.

Mr Carstairs reluctantly conceded that there was more to their story than he'd thought. "This is the nearest thing to proof you've given me so far," he said.

Tom was struck by an idea. "Look, Mr Fox wants to expel us so he's writing to our parents. Why don't we follow Mr Fox's example and write to Orcon and Porcon's parents and ask them to take them away?"

"Do they have parents?" asked Miles, dismally. "I can't imagine they do. They probably just have pods as parents."

"No, they do have parents," said Asquith Minor, excitedly. "They've told me about them. And they mentioned wanting their claws clipped, too. It's something that their dad won't do yet, even though other dads do. But I remember them telling me he's very strict apparently. Perhaps that's why they wanted to run away for a while?"

Mr Carstairs was pacing the room. The Bros record had stuck and was driving Tom mad. "Can I …?" he said, gesturing to the record player.

"Oh, certainly," said Mr Carstairs. "Put on something sensible, will you? Like some Bach. To be honest I can think better with Bach. Not that Bros aren't – er – def, def, def," he added.

What seemed like hours passed as they waited for Mr Carstairs to work out the instructions and figures. Finally he said, "Look, kids. All I can do is to send their parents a message. But would that be wise?"

"We might be invaded by people from outer space and be made into their slaves!" moaned Asquith Minor, still thinking about the planet Or. Or was it Er? "We might have to eat metal and paddle about!"

"If Orcon and Porcon can get down here," said Mr Carstairs, having thought about it sensibly, "then anyone can. The other inhabitants of Er must have chosen not to visit Earth for some reason or other."

"Is it worth the risk?" asked Susan.

"Of course," said Mr Carstairs, decisively, getting up from his chair. "It's always worth the risk if it's right. And if it's true Mr Fox has expelled you when Orcon and Porcon ought to be expelled, then we must fight for right. Think of Nelson Mandela, after all. Think of the Birmingham Six. We must never rest in the fight for truth and justice."

None of them quite knew why Mr Carstairs was thinking of Nelson Mandela or the Birmingham Six, but they all assumed they must be OK.

"Down with fascist spaceboys! Up the revolution!" added Mr Carstairs. "To the nerve-centre of Burlap Hall!" And they all trooped down the corridor to the computer room where, with great care and anxiety, Mr Carstairs tried to send a message to the planet Er. He addressed it simply "TO THE PARENTS OF ORCON AND PORCON". Then he typed: "YOUR KIDS CAUSING HAVOC ON EARTH STOP PLEASE COLLECT IMMEDIATELY STOP VERY URGENT STOP CARSTAIRS".

CHAPTER NINE

Mr and Mrs Buxton were astonished to get the letter from Mr Fox. They discussed it in the car on their way to Burlap Hall.

"It sounds as if Tom's in serious trouble," said Mrs Buxton, for the twentieth time. "I know Tom's no saint, but he doesn't take drugs, he's no lazier than any other boy ..."

"He's excellent at games, he's polite, he's hard-working," said Mr Buxton. "Did you say left at Ganthold, dear?"

"No, right at Ganthold, left at Upper Peaswick," said Mrs Buxton, staring at the map. "At least, I think so. Let me turn the map round ... I seem to remember we got lost round here last time ..."

"Let's hear that letter once more," said Mr Buxton.

Mrs Buxton got it out of her bag. "'Dear Mr and Mrs Buxton'," she read. "'I have some extremely serious news to impart and I think that for all of us – Tom, myself and you, his parents – it would be best if I could meet you to discuss the situation. Things have been going gravely wrong at Burlap Hall and it seems that Tom is one of the small group of pupils responsible. I trust you will come prepared to take Tom with you when you leave. Yours sincerely, Mr Fox, Headmaster.' It sounds like expulsion to me."

"Ridiculous letter!" scoffed Mr Buxton, turning right. "That man can't even express himself clearly. By the way, should we be on the M42?"

Mrs Buxton put on her glasses and stared at the map. "The M42? Oh no, we should be on the A428!

You must have turned right at Ganthold!"

"You *told* me to turn right!" said Mr Buxton, furiously. "Good God, can't you read a map properly? This is what always happens! Damn, damn, damn! If that ridiculous headmaster had never written that ridiculous letter, we'd never be in this ridiculous situation. God preserve me from headmasters!"

Asquith Minor's parents weren't nearly so tolerant. They were already at the school, cornering their son early in an empty classroom.

"Appalling behaviour!" said Mr Asquith. He wore a gold chain round his neck, gold rings on his fingers and he sported the biggest, goldest Rolex watch on the market.

"You're certain to be expelled!" his mother was saying. She was wearing a leather hat, a leather suit and high heels. "After your dad's spent all these years slaving to give you a proper education! At a proper public school! Bang go your chances of being a wine-merchant or a stockbroker, that's all I can say!"

Asquith Minor didn't dare say anything except, in a sad little piping voice, "Sorry!"

"SORRY!" roared his father. "SORRY! Good heavens, you dare stand there having been expelled from this school and just say you're SORRY!"

Asquith Minor never understood why, whenever he said "Sorry" to anyone, it never seemed to be enough. What else could he say? If he *didn't* say sorry, then they'd only accuse him of not saying sorry. Perhaps saying, "I'm very, very sorry, I wish I could put the clock back, I'll never forgive myself, I'm so sorry" would work. He tried it. But his father just roared back, "You mean to stand there, just telling me you're

VERY, VERY SORRY, YOU WISH YOU COULD PUT THE CLOCK BACK, PLEASE FORGIVE ME, YOU'RE VERY SORRY! HUH!"

Asquith Minor gave up. He said nothing.

"You mean to stand there," roared his father, finally, "just SAYING NOTHING! How dare you!"

Asquith Minor burst into tears.

His mother snorted. "Is that all you can do, just burst into tears?"

Finally Asquith Minor, overwhelmed with despair, put his head in his hands and whispered, "I wish I were dead!"

That fazed his parents only temporarily. After a few minutes his mother snapped back, sarcastically, "And where, pray, do you think that would get you?"

But at least, through his fingers, he saw his father looking rather shocked and signalling to his mother to be quiet. He felt a tiny bit better.

Miles' mother had come on her own and spoke to her son in Mr Fox's waiting room. "For God's sake, darling," she said, "couldn't you have organized this either last week or next week? I was going to Paris today and I've had to put my flight off till tonight. So inconvenient. Couldn't this horrible little man have just put you on a train and sent you home? What's the point of talking it over? I don't want to hear the gory details." She paused, got out her make-up bag and started to put on more lipstick. She scrunched up her lips as if she were saying "Mmmm!" and then licked her teeth with her tongue to see none had stuck. "By the way, what *did* you do? I hope you haven't been chasing girls, like your father." Then another thought struck her and she hastily rummaged around in her bag for a cigarette. "Now, it's nothing to do with drugs, is it?" she said, as she lit it. "Because – " she blew a great gust of cancerous fumes into Miles' face – "because drugs, you know, can kill you."

Susan's parents were too busy at the American Embassy in Rome to make a special trip to England, so her older brother, who worked as the London correspondent for an American newspaper, had been deputed to come and collect her instead. It was a sign of his charm that he'd persuaded Mr Fox to allow Susan to be taken out to lunch in Lanchester before the appointment.

"C'mon, kid, cheer up," he said, noticing how depressed Susan became as they finished their meal. "It's not the end of the world."

Susan sighed. "You'd never believe me if I told you what's *really* happened," she said.

"What?" asked her brother. As a journalist he believed anything that made a good story. His sister explained about Orcon and Porcon and how they came from outer space and how they'd swapped the science block plans for a scheme to build a funfair.

"Outer space!" said her brother, laughing. "Do you ever read a paper called the *Sunday Sport* by any chance? It's full of these great headlines – 'Pensioner chokes on killer sprout', 'Woman, pregnant for 65 years, gives birth to pensioner', 'Is the Queen Mum an alien?'" He thought a bit. "How about 'Scaly students scupper school ...' – or – 'Alien brain-brothers in school downfall scam!'"

"You don't believe me, do you?" said Susan.

"No kidding I don't believe you!" said Susan's brother. "But I can't wait to see these guys Orc and

Porc! You know I always carry my camera around. Maybe I could get some shots of them and sell them to one of the Sunday papers!"

By the time Tom's parents had arrived, half an hour late and furious, Asquith Minor's parents, Susan's brother and Miles' mother were assembled in Mr Fox's waiting room, angrily looking at their watches. Their children were all there as well, looking pale and silent; they weren't looking forward to what Mr Fox would have to say.

Susan's brother glanced out of the window. He frowned as he saw the builders' work. "Hey, kid," he said to Susan, "I see what you mean! Certainly looks like a funfair. They're starting to build coconut shies and hoopla stalls. Crazy!" He started loading his camera. He adjusted the light meter and, lifting the window, leant out and began snapping a quick series of photographs of the builders' work.

Tom and Miles were whispering in the corner. "They'll never come now," said Tom. "Mr Carstairs must have got the message wrong."

"Or if they do come," said Miles, "they'll be terrifying space creatures, all covered with horns and scales and laser beams instead of eyes. They'll probably eat us all for breakfast." Tom felt uncomfortable at the thought.

But their conversation was halted by an astonished gasp from Susan's brother.

"What is it?" asked Susan, looking out of the window. "I can't see anything!"

Susan's brother pulled away from the camera and stared at the lawn, blinking. "Hey, nor can I, like this," he said. "But behind the camera ..." He moved back to peer through the lens. "Wow! Jeez! This is amazing!" He continued snapping faster than ever. Within seconds he'd run out of film and had to put the camera down to break open a new pack. "What's happening?" asked Tom, coming over.

"There are people out there! Well, kinda people. But you can't see them through the window, just through the camera. Must be something to do with the filter! A kinda space-craft ..."

Tom picked up the empty camera and had a look. He nearly had a heart attack. Because there, on the lawn, with a huge twisted aerial and great lights flashing, was an enormous flying saucer. He just had time to see the door of the space-ship open and two hazy figures emerge when Susan's brother snatched the camera back and clicked the new film into place. He put it to his eye. "Jesus H ... *look at that!*" he said.

"What?" said Miles, coming over with Asquith Minor. "Let's see!"

But at that moment, Mr Fox came into the room. Susan's brother continued snapping but the children reluctantly turned to face the headmaster. Fatter and redder than usual, he looked under particular strain – as indeed he was, since voluntarily discarding the termly fees of four pupils with no prospect of their being replaced was, for him, an agonizing decision to have to take. He felt like a sick man told by his doctor that his only chance of survival is to have a foot chopped off. Still, it had to be done. He gritted his teeth and prepared to do the ghastly deed.

"Ah, you're all here! I'm sorry to have kept you waiting."

Asquith Minor looked up. Was his father going to roar SORRY! at Mr Fox? It seemed not. He couldn't understand it. It was something to do with when *he* said sorry. He heard his father saying, greasily, "Not at all, Headmaster!" Asquith Minor shook his head, baffled.

"But," said Mr Fox, "I have been held up. The local education authority on the line. A disaster. Your children have a lot to answer for."

Susan's brother had stopped taking photos, but kept staring out of the window, shell-shocked by what he'd seen.

He whispered to Susan. She started to smile and clapped her hands. "I told you!" she said to him. "But you wouldn't believe me!" Then she whispered to Tom, Miles and Asquith Minor. "It was a flying saucer! And a couple of people, well, kinda people, got off! It must be Orcon and Porcon's mom and pop!"

"You see?" said Mr Fox, turning to the group of children who were now all whispering and looking round. "You see how they behave? How can I run my school with this sort of thing going—" but his speech was interrupted by a knock on the door.

"Come in!" he said, crossly.

And in came two of the strangest creatures any of them had ever seen.

They were *sort* of human-looking, but there again, sort of not. One had long thin hair, a big face, huge eyes, large breasts and was wearing a suit with a tie; the other was of similar height but sported a big moustache and wore a longish skirt topped by a blouse. He – or she – also wore a huge string of pearls around his or her neck. Both of them wore woolly gloves. The whole room fell silent as parents and children alike gawped at the bizarre pair.

The couple were equally dumbstruck as they each

took in the people in the room. Finally the one in the suit whispered to the other, "I toldst thou! The youths and aged men trouser'd are and the damsels sport gowns! Why dost thou never harkest to me?"

"Quiet, prithee, wench!" said the one with the moustache in a skirt.

"And who, may I ask," said Mr Fox in a complete fury, "are you? And what do you mean, coming into my school dressed like that?"

The one with a moustache clapped a hand to his forehead. "Our language! 'Tis all awry!" He reached into the buttons on his blouse and twiddled about while Mrs Asquith gasped in horror. His besuited wife did the same, fumbling inside her waistcoat.

"I'm so sorry," he said, eventually. "Bit of trouble there. Let me introduce ourselves. We are Orcon and Porcon's parents and I gather you've been having a bit of a problem with our kids."

"Orcon and Porcon's parents!" said Mr Fox, reeling back. He was stricken with a mixture of emotion. He wanted to order them out of his school for appearing uninvited and talking weird gothic-speak while dressed in the most ridiculous clothes he'd ever seen; at the same time he was convinced they were very, very rich and could contribute to the science block. He also needed their school fees which were normally paid in advance. Financial considerations finally got the better of him and he recovered himself. He gave his oiliest smile and extended a hand to their gloved ones. "Delighted! Delighted to meet you! I was starting to believe you didn't exist! I have been trying so hard to get in touch with you! The science block! Perhaps Orcon and Porcon told you about it?"

From the clicking sound in the corner, Tom knew

148

that Susan's brother wasn't wasting a moment. Miles whispered, "The spaceboys' mum and dad! Although the way they're dressed they probably call them Mad and Dum!" Asquith Minor burst into a fit of giggles, much to the disapproval of his parents.

"Far from your children causing trouble," said Mr Fox, rubbing his hands, "they set an example to all our pupils."

Orcon's father – or rather, the one in the dress – looked puzzled. "Knowing them as I do," he said, "I doubt it, somehow. They've got themselves into this kind of scrape before. And anyway, if they're so brilliant why did we receive this?" He handed Mr Fox a piece of paper. The headmaster read it aloud, scratching his head.

"'Your kids causing havoc on earth. Please collect immediately. Very urgent. Carstairs.' Carstairs! He sent you this! I shall ask him to explain himself immediately! Buxton! Go and fetch Mr Carstairs immediately!"

Miles' mother was sighing and looking at her watch. "Mr Fox," she said, "we have waited nearly half an hour to see you. I have a plane to catch. Could we start this interview now?"

"Dear lady," said Mr Fox, taking her hand and pressing it. "Forgive me. If you can wait just a few moments while I sort out this little matter … it won't take long."

Tom, panting, brought Mr Carstairs to the headmaster. The English teacher scanned the room until his eyes fell on the spaceparents. He didn't hesitate but bounded up to them and pumped their woolly hands with a hearty, "Hello! So you got my note! Brill! Def! Great to meet you! Carstairs is the name!"

One of Mr Fox's famous "looks" started to spread

over his face. His ears were twitching dangerously and his neck began to swell. "Ah, Carstairs! So you don't deny you sent this note! I have a bone to pick with you! Orcon and Porcon are our star pupils! I am shocked!"

Mr Carstairs grinned. "I think the word 'star' is actually more correct than you imagine," he said. "They come, you see, from the stars." Mr Fox turned to Orcon's parents to apologize for this ridiculous statement but was horrified to find them nodding in agreement. "I think," he said, in huffy confusion, "we had better discuss this in private." And with that, he ushered them into his study.

"Could I suggest that Tom, Miles, Susan and Asquith Minor come too?" asked Mr Carstairs. "You see they're really more into this than I am. They know Orcon and Porcon intimately. They know exactly what they've been up to."

"I hardly think that these ..."

But Orcon's mum (or was it dad) leant forward, smiling. "Yes, that's right. Come on in," she said. "You can tell us what's been going on with our two tearaways."

"Tearaways!" said Mr Fox as he went into his office. "I'd hardly call them that!"

"I would," said Orcon's dad grimly as they shut the door.

CHAPTER TEN

"Now what's all this about?" Mr Fox sat down irritably behind his desk. "I have several parents to see and they're getting impatient. Parents with appointments," he added, looking meaningfully at Orcon and Porcon's mother and father, implying that they *hadn't* got an appointment.

Orcon's dad cleared his alien throat, smoothed his skirt and started. "We come from the planet Er," he began.

Mr Fox interrupted him.

"Now look here," he said. "I don't want some cock and bull story, Mr, er, Orcon. I want to hear what this is all about."

Orcon's father's face reminded Tom of the space-boys' expressions when they were angry.

"I assure you, this is no cock and bull story. I would be grateful if you would hear me out," said Orcon's father. He fiddled crossly with the string of pearls round his neck. "As I was saying – before you interrupted me – we come from the planet Er. My sons, Orcon and Porcon, have a nasty habit of tinkering around with our computers and our space waves, creating havoc, as Mr Carstairs so aptly put it, on other planets.

"Last year they ran away to Vanath and practically closed down their nuclear life farms; then there was the escapade to Dern – they washed the ozone layer there till it shrank, and then used it as a blanket! You can imagine how the government of Dern felt about us. It took a great deal of time and money to get things back to normal."

"It's my fault," said Orcon's mother, adjusting her tie. "I'm too soft on them. But things are going to change from now on. No more four-dimensional television for at least a fortnight."

"And we'll have to get their claws clipped, finally," said Orcon's father. "On our planet," he explained, turning to Mr Fox, "when boys get to Orcon and Porcon's age they often behave very badly until their claws are clipped, when they usually settle down and become more responsible. But people are clipping children's claws earlier and earlier these days and I'm of a generation that doesn't believe in it being done too early. I'm sure you have similar problems of behaviour with teenagers on this planet."

"Teenagers!" said Mr Fox, clutching on to the only bit of this speech he understood. "Teenagers! You won't believe what some of our teenagers have done here! They've spat at the examiners, they've sung rude songs, they've behaved atrociously. And, as a result, there's a real chance this school will be closed down! In fact, it's only your two boys who give me any hope. They're brilliant. We've entered them as our school's group in a national computer competition and they've nearly won."

Orcon's father looked rather shifty, picking embarrassedly at the brooch on his blouse. "Mr Fox, I'm afraid that it's most likely it's our boys who've *made* your pupils behave badly. It's good fun, you see, for kids at that age. I remember I was just like them myself. But I grew out of it – after my claws were clipped, of course." At the mention of "claws" Mr Fox surreptitiously eyed Orcon's father's woollen gloves. "But of course in those days things didn't have such serious consequences. We didn't have such powers at our disposal when we were young. We were quite happy then, with a couple of neuron waves and a time machine. Ah, those simple pleasures! And anyway, we would never have dreamt of running off to other planets."

"Yes, the good old days," said Orcon's mother, sighing. "We had good manners in those days. And a visit to the intergalactic 5D cinema cost less than 1000 zots a ticket."

"*And* you still got change, even when you'd bought a bag of bolts to eat while watching," said Orcon's dad wistfully. "But enough of this nostalgia. Are these the kids who've suffered at the hands of ours?" He gestured towards Tom, Miles, Susan and Asquith Minor who were sitting goggled-eyed at all this; indeed, if only ears could goggle they would have been goggle-eared as well.

"Yes," said Susan. "It was awful. One boy was made to pour water over Mr Fox, a girl was forced to chip 'Mr Fox is a complete nerd' into the panelling ..."

"Where?" said Mr Fox, leaning forward sharply. "I never saw it!"

"And we've been made to stick our tongues out and our brains have been emptied of knowledge, and we've had to sing rude songs – it's been awful," added Asquith Minor. "And my parents are furious!"

Mr Fox looked incredulous. He turned to the English teacher. "Carstairs," he said, "you don't believe any of this poppycock, do you?"

Mr Carstairs nodded his head regretfully. "I'm afraid I do, Headmaster," he said. "I've seen the Apple program Orcon and Porcon made to get them back to Er."

"Apples! We're not talking about fruit again, are we?"

"No, Headmaster. Apples."

Mr Fox sighed. "Am I the only sane person here? Have all of you been reading the *Sunday Sport*?" Then he corrected himself. He realized he shouldn't have given his Sunday reading habits away. "Whatever that may be," he added, hastily.

Meanwhile Orcon's parents were whispering between themselves; Orcon's mother nodded.

"I think the only way you'll believe us," said Orcon's father, "is if we demonstrate our powers on you so you can see how our children have dominated your pupils. Might I ask how old you are?"

"How old I am? What has that got to do with it?" Mr Fox was outraged. And then he remembered he wanted to ask them to donate money to the science block; it wouldn't do to get on the wrong side of them. He tried to calm down. "Oh, very well, everyone knows. I'm fifty-five."

"Excellent!" said Orcon's father. "I am older than you – one hundred and fifty-seven to be exact. May I try a little experiment?"

"Certainly," said Mr Fox. "But you can't play any tricks on me, I assure you." He sat back twiddling his fingers rather smugly, a confident smile on his face.

"This is no trick," said Orcon's father, leaning forward and fixing Mr Fox with a laser-beam gaze. His eyes glowed like two headlights in a dark tunnel, and then great red beams shot out, flashing with sparks and searing into Mr Fox's eyes. There was a long pause and everyone held their breath.

Tom was on the edge of his seat. Even though he had little sympathy with the headmaster, he couldn't help feeling frightened for him. After all, Orcon's father was an adult; he was *really* powerful. If he felt like it, no doubt he could get Mr Fox to do *anything*.

Meanwhle, Mr Fox's eyes had glazed over. Slowly he stood up. His expression was dead, as if every bit of life had been wiped from his face. His movements were very slow and deliberate as if he were following an instruction manual. Then, with a lot of huffing and puffing, he carefully pulled his desk to one side, took off his shoes and socks and rolled up his trousers. He removed his jacket, pushed up the sleeves of his shirt and, taking a handkerchief from his pocket, tied four knots in the corners and popped it on to his balding head like a hat. Standing in the centre of the carpet as if it were a stage, he looked slowly round, checking that everything was in order. Next, he clapped his hands rhythmically, muttering, "One-two-three-four!" under his breath. Then he put his hands on his hips and started singing.

"Oh, I *do* like to be beside the seaside," he sang, his legs kicking playfully from side to side like a can-can girl. "Oh I *do* like to be beside the sea! Oh I *do* like to walk along the prom, prom, prom where the brass bands play tiddely om pom pom, oh, I *do* – come on everybody, join in!" he cried, pulling Susan and Mr Carstairs up. "Come on, have fun, we're by the sea! All together now – Oh I *do* like to be beside the seaside, I do like to be ...!"

Tom, Miles and Asquith Minor couldn't believe their eyes. On and on the headmaster danced and on and on he sang, until he started to puff and pant as his dancing and singing became faster and more furious.

Finally, Orcon's father clapped his hands and Mr Fox fell in a tumbled, sweating heap on the carpet, looking completely dazed. Rubbing his eyes, he stared round in astonishment; then, realizing he had no shoes or socks on and that his trousers were rolled up to his knees, he scrambled to his feet in a frenzy of embarrassment.

"My goodness!" he gasped. "What have I been doing?" He searched about for his socks and shoes and tried to get himself together. He got dressed hastily, hurriedly pulled his desk back into position and sat down behind it, trying to appear dignified. Unfortunately he had forgotten about the handkerchief on his head and no one liked to point it out to him.

"An unforgivable display," he said, looking round, red in the face. "I can't think what came over me."

"What came over you," said Orcon's father, completely serious, "is what came over these poor pupils of yours when my boys arrived. They are not to be blamed for their behaviour. My boys are." He leant back, crossing his legs and patting his hair.

Mr Fox looked stunned. "But – but – I was going to expel them!"

"Quite. It is Orcon and Porcon who should be expelled."

"And, as a result of all this, my school's going to be closed down!"

Then Tom burst in. "And they've altered the plans to make the science block into a funfair!"

"You wouldn't believe us, Mr Fox," said Susan, "but it's true! They're putting up the Big Wheel now!"

Mr Fox stared at the children in disbelief. Then he got up and went to the window. He looked out – and saw for himself. A funfair! It was clear as day. He'd be the laughing stock of the Headmasters' Association! And what pupil would ever have any respect for him again? Not to mention all that money down the drain! His grand science block plans had been converted into a cheap funfair! What would Nutter say? Instead of a physics room, all Nutter would see was a Hall of Mirrors! In place of a chemistry lab, a Whizzing Waltzer. No space for intricate experiments, just a Tunnel of Love. The humiliation! He staggered back to his chair, sat down, put his head in his hands and groaned – but finding, to his surprise, that he was wearing the knotted handkerchief, he hastily removed it and stuffed it into his pocket.

"My science block!" he moaned. "Now the Education Authority will *never* let me stay on as head-master!"

Everyone in the room was silent. Even the children, witnessing his sudden change from an irritable bag of bluff and pomposity to a moaning heap of distress, couldn't help feeling sorry for Mr Fox. They looked at each other helplessly.

Then suddenly Tom had an idea. "Sir!" he said, "I mean, er, Orcon's father, whatever you're called. Can this power you've got be used to good as well as bad? You said you put right the ozone layer on the planet Dern. Surely if you could do that, you could help Burlap Hall?"

"It's hardly such an important issue," said Orcon's father, reluctantly. ("Not important!" wailed Mr Fox to himself. "How can you say that?") "But I'm sure I could make some recompense." He put his woolly fingers together, to concentrate better. "Just tell me how."

"The science block!" cried Mr Fox, desperately. "If you could just give us some money for the science block!"

Orcon's father rose and, lifting his long skirts, moved to the window. He stared out thoughtfully. Then he spoke. "I can do better than that," he said. "Unless those workmen are very ancient, I can force them to work at ten times the speed for a period of a few days, perhaps. Which means a new science block could be erected within the week. And when I say a new science block," he added, his eyes flashing, "I mean a new science block! Something so modern and incredible that no one will ever have seen anything like it before! Not just a row of old Bunsen burners!"

"A row of old Bunsen burners would be fine!" said Mr Fox, pathetically. "Anything!"

Orcon's mother slapped her thighs jovially. "Perhaps there's something else we could do for you? It's so simple for us, you see."

Mr Fox looked round him wildly. "I can't really think ... You see this inspector, Clive Nutter, and his boss are coming next week to re-inspect the school. I know he'll fail it, even if the pupils are up to standard."

"Oh dear," said Orcon's mother, looking up at her husband who was tutting over a ladder he'd found in one of his stockings. "Couldn't you do something? You could make the pupils clever and polite couldn't you? Just for a while?"

Orcon's father pursed his lips and paced the room, frowning and thinking deeply. Mr Fox was staring at him as if he were the Messiah returned to earth; the children were gazing worriedly and Mr Carstairs had that eager "Come on, you can do it!" look on his face as if he were silently trying to cheer on a horse he'd backed.

Then Orcon's father spoke. "There are so many

pupils, that's the problem," he said. "But I suppose I could time it. Yes! Bring me the classes and I'll hypnotize them into being extremely polite and brilliant for the day that the inspector is due! I'm sure that can be managed. And now, if that is all, I'd like to see my boys and take them away. After I've performed my necessary tasks, that is."

"You can't take them away," said Mr Carstairs, seized with anxiety. "They're due at Lanchester Computer Centre in an hour! To win our prize!"

"Couldn't someone else go?" said Orcon's father, tetchily. "I've got a local Planetary Watch committee I've got to attend. Awfully boring, but one's got to do one's bit. You see there've been all these ray gun assaults recently, and people can't sleep easily in their pods at night."

"Pods!" exclaimed Miles. "I knew pods came into it somewhere."

Orcon's mother turned to the children kindly. "Oh yes, they're very comfortable. You must pop up and try one some day."

"N-no thanks. Or maybe when I'm older," said Miles, not wanting to offend her.

"Why can't these children go instead?" asked Orcon's father, gesturing towards Miles, Tom, Susan and Asquith Minor.

"Because they know very little about computers," said Mr Carstairs.

"Asquith Minor knows a little because he's been helped by your boys. But I'm afraid even he will never grasp the Bit, the Baud and the Byte. Nor, indeed, the Pixcel."

"We'll soon fix that!" said Orcon's father. He turned his glimmering eyes on them and stared. As the red laser beams bored into his head, Tom's knees turned to jelly. It was an even worse feeling than when Porcon looked at him. He could feel the information being forced into his brain, like a giant injection and his head felt as if it would burst.

"My goodness, you're right," added Orcon's father as he continued to stare. "They don't know much, do they? Well," he said finally, turning his gaze off, "that should keep them going for the afternoon. I defy anyone to win any prize over this group!"

Tom, Miles, Susan and Asquith Minor blinked. Suddenly they knew an awful lot about computers. Their heads were filled with fascinating figures. Microchips, modems, systems analysis, it all seemed easy as ABC.

"Right, that's this lot done. Now, I must deal with the science block. After you've taken care of your appointments, please introduce me to the workmen. My apologies, again, for the trouble our boys have caused. Talking of which, where are they?"

At that very moment there was a knock on the door. "Come in!" called Mr Fox as the door opened – and there stood Orcon and Porcon.

Their greenish faces were flushed and excited as if they'd been up to some fresh devilry and they stood giggling and nudging each other. "We've come to go off to the computer competit —" started Orcon. And then he saw his father. His huge watery eyes got even bigger and his wispy hair started wriggling uncomfortably on his head. "Oh, gosh. Oh, Dad."

"Oh, Mum," said Porcon, looking extremely guilty and turning a deep shade of green. They both stared at the floor, twisting their woollen gloves. Their legs seemed to bend and they seemed suddenly shorter than usual. "We can explain everything ..."

"Oh, boys!" said Orcon's mother, getting up, rushing towards them and hugging them to her hairy jacket. "You're bad, bad boys, but I'm so glad to see you! Thank goodness you're safe! We've been so worried! We thought the intergalactic spacetrons had got you! Or that you'd fallen into a black hole!"

Orcon's father was more severe. "Everything has already been explained," he said, icily. "Your mother and I have been worried sick. We've had the space-force out, every computer has been notified of your absence and I even contacted my old friend, head of the Stratoscope department, to keep a special look-out.

"I am ashamed of you two. You have let down us, your parents, you have let down the planet Er and you have let yourselves down ..." ("Same old rubbish," whispered Miles to Tom) "... let down the inter-galactic mission, the Stratospheric hemisphere, let down the global taskforce and have generally been a discredit to nuclear life-forms ..."

Orcon and Porcon looked so utterly dejected that even Tom felt a bit sorry for them. Orcon started crying; drops of green treacly stuff seeped out of his eyes. Porcon kicked him.

"Oh, darling," said Orcon's mother. "Your father doesn't mean it. Do you, dear?"

"I certainly do," said Orcon's father, his eyes flashing furiously. "I think, in fact, that probably the time has come for you boys to have your claws clipped."

Tom winced, worried that Orcon and Porcon would both cry in unison at this news – but to his surprise they cheered up.

"Claws clipped? Great!" said Porcon. His hairs wiggled enthusiastically. "At last! Then we can be

161

spacemen and not spaceboys, we can drink nuclear alcohol without a licence and if we want we can weld with the spacegirls! I knew you'd see reason eventually."

"Yes, honestly, Dad, *everyone* else had their claws clipped months ago," said Orcon, jumping up and down and clapping his gloved hands. "We kept telling you we had grown up but you wouldn't listen!"

"Typical parents!" said Asquith Minor, spontaneously sympathetic.

Orcon's father whirled round angrily.

"What did you say?" he asked, angrily. "Do you want me to build this science block or not?"

"Yes, yes," intervened Mr Fox, scowling at Asquith Minor. "Boys will be boys. I'm sure when Asquith Minor's claws are clipped ... I mean, er ... when he grows up, he'll be just as responsible ... I mean ..."

Orcon's father had turned again to his children. "Now, we won't mention this any more. But you must promise us you will never be so stupid again."

"No, no!" cried Orcon. "Hey, Porcs! We're going home! Did you store Hemisphere Street on television for us? And Space Neighbours?"

"Of course I did," said Orcon's mother, giving them a hug. "But you can't watch them for a fortnight. And I mean it."

"Oh, Mu-um ..." wailed Orcon.

"Well, maybe a week," said Orcon's mother.

"A week!" said Porcon. "We can't wait a week! *Everyone* else will have seen all the episodes!"

"We-ell ..." said Orcon's mother.

"Oh, please, please, Mum, we'll never run away again, we promise ..."

"Well, we'll see," said Orcon's mother, finally giving

in.

"Great! Mum, can we have nails and spanners for supper tonight?"

"With loads of iron filings?" said Porcon. "We're starving!"

"Of course, boys," said Orcon's mother. She turned to Mr Fox. "We're so sorry," she said. "Our boys *have* been a nuisance. But we'll make it up to you, I promise."

"I can't tell you how grateful I am," said Mr Fox, rising to his feet and kissing Orcon's father's woolly hand – because he was wearing a dress – and patting Orcon's mother bluffly on the back, chap to chap, as the space-parents left him to deal with the normal parents. "I just can't believe it. And," he said, turning to the children with great difficulty, "I am very sorry. I have misjudged you." (Asquith Minor wondered whether to yell SORRY! at him but thought better of it.) "Now, I must speak to your parents and explain the situation."

CHAPTER ELEVEN

The parents were more of a problem than Mr Fox had anticipated. It was extremely difficult to persuade them that they had not, in fact, been summoned to take their children away from the school. And, in order not to lose face completely, Mr Fox was compelled to use all his powers to dodge questions and weave complete fantasies in order to calm the parents down. He decided to make out that the intention of the letters had been to ask them to come and take their children to the Lanchester Computer Centre where the competition was being held.

Miles' mother was furious when she found she'd been summoned for no reason other than to give Miles a lift. Luckily for Mr Fox she hadn't brought his letter with her, so he was able to bluff his way out of that one.

"I'm sure that when you get back and read it you will see that it was perfectly clear," he said, hoping someone had thrown it away in the meantime.

"But why couldn't you have organized transport?" she said. "Hired a bus!"

"My dear lady, I knew you would want to experience the pride and pleasure of witnessing your son being part of the school group that won the computer contest. It's a prestigious award, I can tell you."

As Miles' mother had never experienced much pride or pleasure in her son, this was a new feeling for her. But it still didn't take away the irritation she felt at having had to put off her flight.

Susan's brother presented a different problem. He

kept taking snaps of Mr Fox and asking him for quotes. Mr Fox refused to be drawn.

"They're from outer space, aren't they?" Susan's brother kept saying. "This is a fantastic story! How do you feel about it? What did they say?"

"The affairs of my other pupils must remain in complete confidence," said Mr Fox, edgily. "Now, about your sister. There is a computer competition this afternoon and I've summoned you ..."

"Forget the computer competition! What planet are they from?"

"Er – I have nothing to say," said Mr Fox, little realizing how much he had given away with the mention of Er. "No comment. I cannot discuss it. We are just good friends."

Mr and Mrs Buxton were the most difficult to deal with. Mrs Buxton read the letter aloud to Mr Fox.

"You said it was 'a very serious matter'," she said, challengingly.

"What could be more serious – serious and splendid – than getting into the finals of the computer competition? A seriously splendid achievement!" Mr Fox bluffed wildly.

"But look – you say 'Things have been going seriously wrong at Burlap Hall and it seems that Tom is one of the small group of pupils responsible.'"

Mr Fox feigned puzzlement and leant forward.

"Let me see that." He took it from her and thought on his feet as he pretended to read it. "Good heavens, no wonder you were worried. My secretary! I'll have to have a word with her. No, what it was *meant* to say was – 'Tom is one of the small group of pupils responsible – for getting Burlap Hall out of the difficulties it is experiencing. Much to my delight he is part of a group who have reached the computer finals for a competition sponsored by *DATA! DATA!* the well-known computer magazine. He will be attending this ceremony on Wednesday and must find transport to get to Lanchester Computer Centre'. Then we go on to 'trust you will come prepared to take Tom with you when you leave.'" Mr Fox breathed a sigh. He was fairly sure he'd got away with it.

Luckily, Mr and Mrs Buxton were too relieved to find their son hadn't been expelled to spot any small errors in his story, and after Mr Fox had gone on for about ten minutes telling them what a genius Tom was, how polite, charming, talented he had turned out, they felt like stiff new shoes which had been punched and pummelled and walked on and bent till they were now flexible and soft and comfortable. They had been flattered into submission.

Asquith Minor's parents, who were excessively impressed by any achievement which involved certificates, needed no such buttering up. They were simply astonished and proud to hear their son had achieved anything at all.

"Wait till we tell the Parkinsons," said Mrs Asquith to her husband as they left Mr Fox's office. "Their son hasn't won anything, ever!" As they went off, Mrs Asquith even gave her son a kiss, much to his astonishment.

Orcon's father started his work with the science block. Gathering up his skirts, he asked to be taken to the spot where the construction was taking place and followed Mr Fox down the gravel paths to the building

166

site. He wobbled slightly on his high heels over the stones and had to be held up by Mr Carstairs. Orcon's mother strode beside him in her suit, her children at her side.

As he observed the sorry state of the grounds, Orcon's father felt compelled to comment. "Forgive my asking," he said, "but is there anything else you would like me to do? It's no trouble for me. Don't hesitate to ask."

Mr Fox paused. He knew how badly the grounds needed doing. "Maybe you could give those hedges a trim," he said, pointing.

"With what?" asked Orcon's father.

"With these," said Mr Fox, picking up a pair of clippers that lay nearby. Orcon's father stared at Mr Fox and within seconds the headmaster was hurtling along the hedges chopping them back like a character from a silent movie. Sweat dripped from his brow and he gasped for breath, but still he clipped and clipped until all the hedges surrounding the lawn were looking neater and sprucer than they had in ages.

"Perhaps he should mow the lawn as well, while he's at it," suggested Mr Carstairs, who was accompanying them.

"Good idea. Most untidy," said Orcon's father, staring at Mr Fox again before he had a say in the matter. With a stifled howl poor Mr Fox scampered towards a shed, hauled out the lawnmower and mowed the enormous lawn – in one minute.

Mr Fox came out of the trance exhausted, falling down at their feet on the gravel and lying there, gasping into the stones. His suit was covered in grass-stains, his hands were blistered with clipping and four leaves rested among his few hairs, giving his head the air of a Roman emperor.

"Bit of exercise!" smiled Orcon's father, pulling him up. "Does you good! Now, the builders. Kids," he added to Orcon and Porcon, "while I'm sorting them out, continue with the grounds, will you?" The space-boys instantly sprang into action; they raced away, lopping trees, plucking dandelions from the paths, neatening the borders of the lawn and clearing patches of weeds.

Alf, Fred and Bill were, as usual, taking a long tea-break. They were playing cards on a log, although each had his hand on a tool, ready to spring into action if anyone came by. Orcon's father looked at the plans, asked for a pencil, and briefly sketched out new plans on the back of the old ones. Everything was entirely accurate as he drew lengths, measurements, widths, angles – even specifying the exact material that was to be used. Inner and outer joists, plumbing, heating – everything was lined up and listed with a few strokes of the pencil.

"Now, let's get these builders going," he said. "A week of non-stop work. That should do the trick." He stood with his arms folded, glaring at the builders with his eyes and boring into them with his laser stare.

Slowly the three men started to move, getting quicker and quicker until, eventually, they were nothing more than a blur of activity. Within a few minutes the funfair structure had been ripped down, and the builders got to work on the new science block. Alf bent metal with his bare hands; Fred used his teeth and feet as well as his hands to build a wall. Bill checked the new plans and altered all the old materials – joists, bricks, slates, cabinets, window frames, stair-cases, carpets, desks, chairs, scientific instruments, books, gutters, drains, wires – to comply with the new plans. Orcon's father nodded. "That's the basic structure now. They'll slow down a little bit from now on but it should be all finished and in working order by June 10th. Anything else?"

"I suppose we couldn't get the whole school decorated and generally repaired, could we?" said Mr Fox, wondering if he wasn't pushing his luck; but after all, he had nothing to lose.

"Certainly," said Orcon's father. "But we need manpower. Assemble the teachers and pupils."

Soon all the pupils and teachers were thronging into the great hall. Orcon's father, having pinned back the large brooch which had come adrift on his blouse, paused. "Now let me get this correct," he said. "It's next Thursday this Nutter is coming, isn't it? June 10th?"

"It's like setting the timer on a video," whispered Susan.

"Exactly," said Orcon's father, overhearing her. "I have to hypnotize you and the other pupils and then program you to be incredibly intelligent, polite, charming and brilliant just for a few hours. I couldn't do it for longer than that. So it's essential I get the date exactly right." He rolled up his floral sleeves, folded his arms and gave the assembled pupils a stare with such bright eyes it seemed as if the entire assembly hall might burn down.

Then he paused and said, "Now, the decoration and repair."

In the nick of time Mr Carstairs scrambled up to the back of the podium, away from the effects of the second stare, pulling Tom, Miles, Susan and Asquith Minor with him. "We can't be busy decorating when

169

we should be winning the competition," he said.

Meanwhile, Orcon's dad gave the entire school a penetrating red stare until all the pupils were so dizzy their ankles felt like jellies.

But they swiftly recovered and soon everyone was busy. Some were up ladders, painting away nineteen to the dozen. Miss Shepherd did the kitchens single-handed, while Signor Ruzzi fitted new cookers and sinks provided by Orcon's father; Mr Roy was responsible for the corridors – and Mrs Grain recarpeted the place from top to bottom. Half the pupils rushed round doing the classrooms and studies, repairing broken window frames, painting over the graffiti in the loos, cleaning out and re-adjusting the boilers, adding damp-proof courses and replastering where needed; the other half made new curtains and chair-covers, re-wired the school and put in new sockets for lamps and gadgets.

As this was going on, Mr Fox (who had also shrewdly stood *behind* Orcon's father) whispered to Mr Carstairs, "Oh dear, what do you think of the colour?"

"Def," said Mr Carstairs, firmly. True, the school was being painted a terrible kingfisher blue with orange gloss on the woodwork, but they could hardly ask Orcon's father to start his hypnotizing again. Luckily Orcon's mother came to their rescue. She stuck her thumbs into her waistcoat and reviewed the scene.

"I don't think, dear, that it's a suitable colour for a school," she said to her husband. Then she got out a large briar pipe and tapped it into her hand thoughtfully. "What about a simple cream and white?"

Orcon's father looked irritated. Taking a small lace handkerchief from one of his pockets he mopped his brow and peered at the sky through one of the large stained-glass windows. "But it's 2.13!" he said. "We don't have time!"

"Just for me, dear," said Orcon's mum, winking slyly at Mr Carstairs and Mr Fox. And Orcon's father resignedly summoned the entire school again and got them to change the colour to cream and white, with dusky grey carpets and dark red linoleum. "And remember the windows," whispered Orcon's mother. "They're filthy."

"And now," said Orcon's father, "it really is time for us to go." He turned to Mr Fox. "Thank you for your hospitality and if you're ever passing the planet Er please look in on us. Mr Carstairs has our address."

"Er – thank you," said Mr Fox, staring round in wonder and amazement as he saw Burlap Hall being transformed before his eyes.

"Now – your computers. I really need them outside while we board the spaceship," said Orcon's father. "But I imagine that might cause problems."

"I'm sure, with extension cables ..." said Mr Carstairs.

"It will be far easier to bring the spaceship into the computer room," said the space-dad.

"But ..." interrupted Mr Fox, thinking of his new ceilings.

"It will cause no damage, I assure you," said Orcon's father. "To the computer room, if you please," he added to Mr Carstairs who led him and his family along the corridor, past Mr Roy who was whizzing along with brushes behind each ear, between his toes, in each hand, in his teeth and under his arms, doing an extraordinary whirling dance like a spinning top, painting perfectly as he moved from one end of the corridor to the other, leaving immaculate white walls behind.

The children followed Mr Carstairs and the space-family; they couldn't miss witnessing their departure.

In the newly-decorated computer room, Orcon's father gave a long piece of paper to Mr Carstairs. "If you would be so kind," he said, "as to program us in while we prepare for take-off. First of all I must summon the saucer."

"We've got lots of saucers in the kitchen," said Mr Fox, eager to help. "And cups."

"No, *the* saucer," explained Orcon's mother, kindly. "Our flying saucer."

Mr Fox's eyes bulged so far out of his head he looked like a Pekinese.

Orcon's father continued, addressing his remarks to Mr Carstairs. "You will see, by the way, that I have included a self-destruct program. You wouldn't want, I'm sure, to find by accident at some later date that you had transported yourself to our planet."

"Good idea," said Mr Carstairs, sitting down at the computer. It was a dreadful prospect.

The space-family solemnly held hands in a ring and started humming. The sound got louder and louder until Tom thought his eardrums would burst. Then, when he could bear it no longer, the flying saucer suddenly materialized in the computer room. And yet materialized wasn't quite the word; it was more as if a film of it had appeared in the room. It was sort of there and sort of not there.

An unearthly ladder sprang out of the door and Orcon and Porcon scrambled up it, followed by their parents. Then they turned and waved. As they stood by the entrance, all with their huge heads, their big, watery eyes, their wispy hair and their gloves, Tom felt a tinge of affection for them – yes, even for Orcon and

Porcon. They were just boys growing up like him, really. OK, they had been horrible, but people could be horrible sometimes and then change. He was glad they were going to get their claws clipped. When Orcon actually smiled at him, he found himself involuntarily smiling back.

Orcon's father leant in front of them and shut the door; a few moments later his big head appeared in the cockpit and he could be seen sitting at the controls, his long ear-rings jiggling as he studied the flashing panel in front of him.

"Start programing us – now!" Orcon's father's voice boomed from a loudspeaker inside the ship. Orcon and Porcon stared out of the windows waving and making faces. Mr Carstairs tapped away at the keyboard like mad. The humming noise started up even louder than before; then there was a flash of green smoke and a tremendous bang – and the space-family was gone.

Tom, Miles, Asquith Minor and Susan took their hands from their ears and rubbed their eyes until the smoke cleared. There was nothing there at all. The computer room was just the same – though the picture of the great spotted woodpecker and the seed dispersal poster had whirled into the air with the pressure and now dropped to the floor. Suddenly Mr Carstairs looked at his watch.

"It's late," he cried. "We'll miss the computer competition! Hurry!"

The competition passed in a blur. Tom could hardly remember anything about it except that his parents rushed him off and when the four children were asked questions by computer boffins he felt tremendous relief as he got rid of all the knowledge that Orcon's father had put into his head.

They all stood on a large platform in front of an audience of everyone who was anyone in Lanchester. With each question he answered correctly, the lighter and freer Tom felt. It was a particularly pleasant feeling, too, being able to see the horrified faces of the pupils of St Beowulf's, who'd come to cheer their team and had so far been unable to contribute a single "Hurrah for St Beowulf's!" the whole afternoon. That would teach them to cheat at cricket.

Finally, there were only two questions left.

"Who," asked the editor of *DATA! DATA!*, clipboard in hand, "designed the original Apple? Mr Core" (laughter) "Mr Cox, Mr Pip" (more laughter) "or none of these?"

"None of these," replied Asquith Minor, quick as a flash. The answers leapt out of his brain like lightning.

"Then, to win the *DATA! DATA!* prize for the Bits, Bauds, Bytes and Pixcels competition, there is only one more question! Name the man who, with Steven G. Wozniak, designed the Apple computer in 1976!"

An answer, as before, came leaping to all their lips – but before Tom spoke, he paused. Could there really be a man called Steven P. Jobs? It sounded dreadfully rude – like one of Orcon and Porcon's final tricks. Still, it was either that or nothing. They all looked at each other, thinking the same thing. Tom started off, hesitantly.

"Steven," he said, looking at the editor.

"Yes ..." said the editor.

"P," put in Miles, tentatively.

"Correct!" said the editor.

"Jobs!" whispered Susan, in a low voice. There was a long silence. Mr Carstairs looked absolutely horrified and hid his face in his hands. Tom thought he was going to be thrown off the podium and sent back to school in disgrace. But a smile spread over the editor's face.

"CORRECT!" he shouted. "May I proclaim – silence please!" – he could hardly be heard above the roars and clapping from the audience – "the winners! Burlap Hall!"

There was uproar. Someone stepped forward with a silvered model of a computer with *DATA! DATA! Winners of the Bits, Bytes, Bauds and Pixels Competition* engraved on it and handed it to Tom, Miles, Susan and Asquith Minor. Flashbulbs from the cameras of local newspaper photographers exploded in their faces; Mr Carstairs received a cheque to buy more computer equipment and everyone clapped and hooted. Even the St Beowulf supporters were forced to raise a congratulatory yell of admiration; if they hadn't they would have had to return to St B's with lots of unshouted cheers all choking inside them.

On the way back (Miles and Susan crammed into the Buxtons' car because Miles' mother had had to catch her plane and Susan's brother had insisted on rushing off to London to try to sell the story of the spaceboys to a Sunday newspaper) none of them could really believe what had happened. "Surely the school will just be the same dreary old building when we get back," said Susan. "It felt like a dream."

"*This* isn't a dream," said Tom, pointing to the prize he was clutching. "It must be true."

"A dream?" laughed Mr Buxton, at the wheel. "Certainly not. It's just that you younger generation find computers so easy. You have absolutely no techno-fear. Marvellous."

The new-look Burlap Hall was still there, painted from top to bottom. There was a smell of new carpets and freshly-cut lino. The windows were gleaming and sparkling; the kitchens looked like something from the Ideal Home exhibition and the cooks were marvelling at the new gadgets they found in all the drawers.

Even the pupils' bedrooms and dormitories had all been freshly painted – and the whole school felt spick and span. Looking out of the window as he waved goodbye to his parents, Tom couldn't believe the state of the grounds – the lawn immaculately cut, the hedges neat and tidy and, behind it all, the sight of a wall of the new science block, rapidly rising before his eyes.

Mr Fox had called a teachers' meeting. After its transformation the teachers' common room looked very different. There was a smart new grey carpet on the floor, old notes stuck up with ancient Sellotape had vanished and in their place, on the gleaming white walls, were ordered sets of delightful prints in shining frames; all the chairs had been re-covered in tasteful chintz, the tables sparkled with polish and the whole room was illuminated by hidden spotlights.

The place was like a luxury hotel, with deep-pile carpet, lifts, intercoms, smoke alarms, sprinklers and every modern gadget imaginable. Those who had been to their own bedrooms before the meeting had been astonished to find springy new matresses, newly covered downy duvets, electric blankets, bedside lights that worked and discreet little basins with hot and cold running water and heart-shaped soaps, packets of moisturisers (for the ladies) and shaving cream (for the men) on the side, hidden cunningly in their cupboards.

Gradually they accepted the explanation offered by

Mr Fox, incredible as it seemed at first.

"And so," said Mr Fox, his eyes blazing with triumph, as he sensed victory in his grasp, "we will, I think, be able to put Mr Clive Nutter thoroughly in his place next Thursday. He is bringing his boss, Bill Babbage, to endorse his views, before embarking on his plans to take over this establishment. But he has reckoned without the spirit of this great school. The pupils will have education pouring out of their ears. They will have so much knowledge that Nutter and Babbage won't know how to cope with it. Ha! I say." He snapped his fingers. "A fig for Nutter and Babbage!"

There was a burble of heartfelt approval from the assembled teachers. Perhaps there really was a chance that Burlap Hall could be saved, Mr. Fox would stay on as headmaster and they'd all keep their jobs?

But in among the hubbub was heard the resonant, precise voice of Mrs Grain. "Talking of Nutter and Babbage," she said, "you did get that phone message I left on your desk when you were out seeing the builders with Orcon and Porcon's father, didn't you?"

"No," said Mr Fox, puzzled. "Why?"

"Oh, nothing important," said Mrs Grain. "They're just coming on June 11th instead of the 10th. That makes no difference, does it?"

The silence that emanated from Mr Fox was deafening. His cheeks bulged, his forehead swelled, a couple of very long hairs on his head managed to rise in horror, and his ears seemed to swivel like revolving bow-ties. He tried to speak, but he couldn't. All that came out of his mouth were muffled sounds, like those a gagged prisoner makes when trying to draw attention to himself.

Mr Carstairs was the first to speak. "No difference!"

he said. "What do you mean no difference? What are we going to do?"

"It's only a day," said Miss Shepherd, puzzled.

Mr Fox finally found a voice. "It makes *all* the difference! Orcon's father has hypnotized the entire school to be bright and brilliant from 9 o'clock to 4 o'clock on Thursday June 10th. By Friday 11th June the hypnosis will have worn off, the children will be back to normal."

Now it was the teachers' turn to be silent. They'd barely got adjusted to the last new situation when suddenly extinction stared them in the face again. Worse, as Signor Ruzzi pointed out with a low moan, "And Meester Nutter – he will be now the one with the new music room, the Steinway piano …"

"And the new kitchens and the new textbooks …" wailed Miss Shepherd.

"And the new sports rooms and the new gym and the new computers," groaned Mr Carstairs.

"Not to mention the new science block," said Mrs Grain, tearfully.

"And the lovely grounds, the bedrooms …" added Mr Roy, his face ashen.

The thought was devastating. But what on earth could they do?

CHAPTER TWELVE

When Mr Fox finally sat down by himself to contemplate the problem, he found it impossible. It was like witnessing a road accident; he had to turn away. It was with an affectionate, sad smile that he noticed the skirting board in his study was still orange – the only tiny flaw in Orcon's father's plan. Everything had been in his grasp – and now it had all slipped away. Worse, his new school would soon be in the hands of his arch enemy. He felt like crying. Pouring a stiff whisky, he summoned Mr Carstairs. He was the only one who could possibly help.

When the English teacher arrived, Mr Fox was struck by his downcast appearance. Mr Carstairs sat in the chair opposite Mr Fox's desk, actually looking as if he never wanted to get out of it again. It was that bad. For Mr Carstairs' part, as he sat dejectedly sipping at the warm whisky Mr Fox had given him, he reflected that when Mr Fox offered drinks to teachers things must be in a very sorry state indeed.

"Mr Carstairs," whispered Mr Fox huskily, trying not to show his emotion. "Can't you do something?"

Mr Carstairs shook his head, sadly. "You must remember that Orcon and Porcon's father deliberately destroyed their return program to stop anything like this happening again," he said. "*They* could get in touch with us, but *we* can never get in touch with them." He sighed deeply. "I suppose you couldn't get Clive Nutter to stick to his original arrangement? Say it would be very inconvenient to change the appointment?"

Mr Fox reached for the telephone. "I'll try, but I hold little hope."

His prediction was correct. The more fiercely Mr Fox argued that it was essential that Clive Nutter arrive on June 10th, the more determined was Nutter to keep to his new plan. He smelt a rat.

"If you can't be flexible, Mr Fox," he said down the end of the phone, sounding as if he had a clothes-peg on the end of his nose, "it will only count against you. One thing modern schools need is flexibility. Flexibility combined, of course, with rigidity," he added, enigmatically.

Mr Fox put down the phone and sighed, shaking his head.

"If this were Nutter's first visit we might get away with it," he mused. "After all, with Orcon and Porcon not here, the children will just be their normal selves. But Nutter is so prejudiced against us now. He only has to hear one wrong answer to confirm everything. And this Babbage man will obviously have been thoroughly primed."

"But the school's looking so good!" said Mr Carstairs, trying to dredge up some enthusiasm.

"Yes, I know. *And* the school group has won the *DATA! DATA!* award. But unless the pupils perform absolutely brilliantly on the day of Nutter's inspection we've got no chance. I know Nutter."

But at the mention of the computer competition Mr Carstairs started forward, struck by an idea. His knees twitched hopefully as if they were preparing to eject him from his seat. "The computer competition!" he said. "Why didn't I think of it! Do you think there's just a small chance that some of the brilliance Orcon's father hypnotized into the kids won't yet be used up?

Maybe they have an answer!"

But he was looking at an empty chair. Mr Fox had already sprung up like a kangaroo, hurtled to the door and was roaring for Tom, Miles, Susan and Asquith Minor at the top of his voice.

"Not so loud!" urged Mr Carstairs, a finger to his lips. "You might break the hypnotism spell!"

It was a very puzzled foursome who were ushered into Mr Fox's study a few minutes later.

But — "It's all gone," said Miles, apologetically. "I don't know a baud from a byte."

Asquith Minor and Susan agreed.

It was only Tom who thought he might have retained a little something — but after scraping around in his memory he gave up. Then he said, "What about approaching this as just a problem, not a computer problem?"

Miles chipped in, "Wasn't there a Friday 13th virus? How did people overcome that?"

Seeing Mr Fox's baffled face, Mr Carstairs explained. "Some joker somehow put an order into a computer program to ensure that on every Friday 13th all the computers linked to the same system would forget various bits of their programs. It had a terrible effect on computers throughout the world, wrecking thousands of programs."

"But how did they stop it?" asked Mr Fox, who was interested in solutions, not problems.

Asquith Minor interrupted. "The only computers that escaped were ones which didn't know there was a Friday 13th."

"Everyone knows there's a Friday 13th," said Mr Fox irritably. He sat back in his chair, drumming his fingers.

"Yes," said Miles, "but if you tell your computer that this month there's no Friday 13th the computer will believe you. And it'll escape being hit by the thing that destroys it."

"You can't just tell a computer there's no Friday 13th," said Mr Fox. "It would know better."

"Ah!" said Mr Carstairs, his knees starting up their rhythmic twitching again. "That's where you're wrong. Computers only do what they're told. And that's why," he added, his knees slowing down again, "it wouldn't work in this case. It's no good saying to all the pupils that there isn't a June 10th. And even if you could it would only mean they'd just miss out June 10th and since all their education and brilliance is going to come out on June 10th, the result would be that they'd just override it."

"And it wouldn't work if you just *told* us that all the information Orcon's father programed into us, to come out on June 10th, should come out on June 11th," added Asquith Minor. "Because Orcon's father has programed us like a computer. He's tapped a part of us we don't know how to get to."

The heavy silence that hung over them all in the study was like a physical presence.

"The only way we could do it," said Tom, suddenly, "would be to *fool* all the pupils that June 11th was June 10th! If they really believed it, really, really believed it, that way I bet it would work!"

Mr Carstairs clapped his hands. "If that's not a def idea, I don't know what is!" he said. "But how? There's no way we can pretend next Friday will be June 10th. Everyone'll know it's the 11th."

"If we were to keep everyone in school," said Tom,

182

excitedly, "and draw the curtains for the next week and not allow anyone out, and keep everyone in artificial light, then couldn't we juggle the hours so that by next week we'd all think Friday was June 10th even though it wasn't? Let's say you got everyone to give in their watches and clocks so they couldn't see the time, and then *you* told them when it was Saturday, Sunday and so on, you could, by making each day a little longer, fool them into thinking that June 11th was the 10th. There'd be twenty-four hours to account for – the difference between Thursday and Friday – so if you divided twenty-four by seven and added that on to each day, about three and a half hours, then by Friday everyone would think it was Thursday."

Mr Fox gulped. He stared at Tom, his eyes boggling. His brain felt full of whirling multiplication tables and division signs and calendars. He had absolutely no idea what the boy was talking about, but he felt, from the way everyone was staring at Tom, that there must be a logic in it somewhere. Mr Carstairs was goggling in amazed admiration. "Are you sure there isn't some of that spell left over?" he was asking. "Let me check this." He got out a bit of paper and started writing "Twenty-four divided by seven ..."

"Do you think it'll work, Carstairs?" asked Mr Fox nervously.

"I think it's *brilliant*," cried Mr Carstairs, having checked Tom's maths. His twitching knees finally launched him from his chair like a rocket and all his old enthusiasm returned. "We must start tonight! Seal up the windows so no daylight can get in, remove everyone's watches and clocks, ban newspapers, radios and televisions and start confusing the pupils as from now! Then tomorrow, wake everyone up three and a half hours later and then the same the next night and so on – brilliant!"

"My thoughts exactly," said Mr Fox. He still didn't understand a word of it. "Now we must get the school together and tell everyone the plan."

Mr Carstairs smacked himself on the forehead so hard he almost knocked himself out. "That's the *last* thing we should do, Headmaster!" he said. "The utmost secrecy is essential! If the pupils know what's going on, they won't be fooled!"

"Precisely," said Mr Fox, totally confused. "Just testing. Right. Not a word of this outside this room."

"I suppose it won't work for us, then," said Asquith Minor, gloomily. He had been rather looking forward to being absolutely brilliant for a day.

"Not necessarily," said Mr Carstairs. "The more we fool ourselves, the more we fool the pupils. And as long as somehow your subconscious, your internal time-clock, believes it's June 10th, that's all that matters. It might work for you lot; it might not."

Organizing the following week was extremely difficult. Some pupils insisted on pulling the curtains away and were muddled when they saw daylight outside when it should be night, and vice-versa. A couple of kids had managed to keep their radios and got very confused by the difference in what time they thought it was at school and what time it said on the radio; but on the whole the operation went reasonably smoothly.

By Friday June 11th, when the curtains were finally drawn in the morning, and watches and clocks returned (properly altered, of course; and Mr Carstairs had kept back the papers and the television off till later that evening) virtually all the pupils were convinced it was, in fact, Thursday 10th June.

It was now just a matter of waiting to see whether the ruse was successful – and, indeed, waiting to see if Orcon's father's hypnotism would actually work. Certainly, none of the pupils had shown any extra politeness or brilliance on the real June 10th and now Mr Fox worried that Orcon's father had conned him.

"Don't worry, Headmaster," said Miss Shepherd at breakfast as she daintily removed the raisins from her muesli ("So bad for the teeth"). "It's quarter to nine, and you said that they weren't hypnotized to be brilliant until nine o'clock."

But Mr Fox was in a terrible state. Clive Nutter and Bill Babbage were due at 9 a.m. and knowing them they might be early. He couldn't eat a scrap of breakfast and he felt physically sick at the idea of them coming round to re-inspect the school. What if none of this worked? What if, despite everything, Bill Babbage decided that Nutter was right and that Mr Fox should be sacked? At one minute to nine, Mr Fox was still a bag of nerves.

His fears, however, were completely unfounded. Because, as Bill Babbage drove himself and Clive Nutter up the school drive in a car that was jerking and sputtering rather awkwardly – Bill Babbage was certain it was the carburettor – Clive Nutter was already looking with horror at the state of the school.

"They've certainly tidied things up since I was here a fortnight ago," he said, peering out of the window at the neat lawns, the clipped hedges, the immaculate tennis courts and the spotless swimming pool with a spanking new diving board glittering above it. The sun was out and the windows of the school were gleaming so brightly he had to blink. As for the paintwork, it was new and sparkling and the ivy that had almost covered most of the windows had been neatly clipped back. The flowerbeds were bursting with blooms, hydrangeas and rhododendrons flowering gaudily. And, worst of all, there was an immaculate new building erected at one side of the school. Through its shimmering panes both Nutter and Babbage could see the escalators, the lifts, the white rooms equipped with telescopes, glass tubes, microscopes and all kinds of electronic machinery. Pupils in white coats were already lined up at their desks and there was no doubt about it: the new science block had risen up in the last week as quickly as mustard and cress.

"I thought you said there wasn't a science block?" said Bill Babbage, suspiciously, as he turned to park on the gravel outside the main gates. "Looks like a science block to me, if ever there was one. Looks like rather a *good* science block, in fact."

"They can't have constructed it so quickly!" said Nutter, rubbing his horrid little eyes.

"No, they can't," said Bill Babbage, thoughtfully, as he put on the handbrake.

"Maybe it's a hologram," said Nutter, rather pathetically, as he prepared to open the car door.

Bill Babbage frowned and stared nervously at Clive Nutter. What an extraordinary thing to say. He, too, reached for the doorhandle, but before either of them could open their doors, they had been pipped to the post by a couple of pupils standing one on either side of the car. Politely they helped the school inspectors out.

"*Ave, magister!*" said Simon. "*Gratus mihi venis!*"

"You what?" said Clive Nutter, clutching his greasy briefcase as he clambered out.

186

"It's Latin, sir," said Simon, "Latin for 'Good morning, sir. I'm glad to see you!'"

"You couldn't be more pleased than I!" said Rosemary. "Welcome to Burlap Hall!"

"Rosemary will take you to Mr Fox's study," said Simon, "while I and a couple of my fellow pupils clean your car. A lovely car, if I may say so, sir; the Austins of 1978 always were better than the later models. But as you drove up I detected you might have a small problem with the carburettor. Would you like our engineering class to have a quick look at it, sir? It would be our pleasure – but of course, if you would prefer to take the car to your own garage, someone here would be glad to make an appointment for you to save you time."

Bill Babbage's jaw dropped. "The carburettor!" he said, goggling. "Yes, I'm sure that's what it is!"

"Yes, sometimes it's a matter of adjusting the fast idle," said Simon. "On most carburettors, when the choke is pulled out, a small cam on the cable opens the throttle to give a fast idle by preventing it from closing to the normal idle position. A small adjustment will soon cure it, I'm sure."

Nodding his astonished agreement, Bill Babbage paused a moment before following Rosemary.

"Before I go – my glasses." He reached inside the glove compartment for his reading spectacles and Rosemary, on the way to Mr Fox's study, enquired, with interest, "I see you're far-sighted, sir. Of course if the eyeball is too short for the focal length of the lens then your eyes must accommodate to get even a distant object properly in focus."

Bill Babbage gawped. He made some joke about getting longer-sighted as he got older.

"Too true, sir," said Rosemary. "It's a sad fact, but the amplitude of accommodation of the human eye diminishes with age. Of course it's because the lens grows less flexible so that its curvature becomes more difficult to vary."

"I'm sure," said Bill Babbage as he climbed the stairs. Then he turned to Clive Nutter. "I thought you said the pupils weren't intelligent, Clive," he said, sharply. "And I thought you said there were no stair-rods on the carpets. Look!" he said pointing over the banisters. "The place is alive with stair-rods!"

"Easy to fix, Bill," said Clive Nutter, nervously. "They probably just went out and bought some the minute I left."

"What?" said Bill Babbage, irritably. But his voice was lost as the harmonies of a great choral work swelled up the stairs in perfect tune. Sopranos, altos, tenors and basses all mingled, now fast, now slow, now loud, now soft. It was a gorgeous cathedral-like sound, a sound to uplift even the most determined non-believers.

"Nice recording," said Bill Babbage. "Mozart?"

Sara, who was coming down the stairs bearing an enormously complicated flower arrangement, attached to which was a label reading "For the old folk of Lanchester, with love from all the pupils of Burlap Hall", stopped. "Excuse me for interrupting, sir," she said. "Forgive my rudeness. But that is actually the Creation, an oratorio by Haydn who died, as you know, in 1809. His works were, of course, based on the style of C.P.E. Bach and he wrote over one hundred symphonies. And that's no recording. It's the school choir. It's just one of many choral works that our music teacher, Signor Ruzzi, is rehearsing for our end of term concert."

At this moment Mr Fox emerged from his study. His step confident, his smile was broad, his shoulders were held back and his whole air was of a man walking tall. He greeted the inspectors with the firm, dry handshake so frequently recommended at the kind of salesmen's seminars entitled, "Close that Deal!" Everything was going smoothly. He was completely reassured that the plan was working. Every child he'd encountered in the last five minutes had been doing things like reciting Chaucer backwards in Chinese, or lecturing on the dangers of cutting down the rainforests or quoting complicated theorems. He felt so utterly confident and puffed-up he even felt more intelligent himself. As he met the inspectors' eyes, his smile became so wide they would have been forgiven for worrying that his face might divide in half. Underneath his gown he had to force his legs to remain straight; his feet felt like skipping and dancing.

"Ah, you've arrived!" he said, almost startled to hear the new resonance in his own voice. "I'm delighted to meet you Mr Babbage. Come in. I was just listening to one of my pupils translating Romeo and Juliet into French. They love to pop in of a morning and practise – you know how it is."

He led them into his study where Susan, blessed with an impeccable French accent, was reading aloud from a book of Shakespeare.

"'O Romeo! Romeo! Pourquoi es-tu Romeo? Renie ton père et abjure ton nom; ou, si cela te répugne, jure de m'aimer toujours, et je renie le sang des Capulets ...' Oh, good morning Mr Nutter. Mr Babbage." She curtsied politely. "I'm afraid I will be in your way. I look forward to seeing you later. Au revoir!"

As he sat down Clive Nutter was speechless. It must be a trick. It couldn't be real. And yet, there was no denying it. As far as the building went, the school was faultless; he had rarely been in such an impeccably kept establishment; the science block, as far as he could see, was up and operating, and the pupils possessed not only incredible manners but seemed to be absolutely bursting with brains and brilliance.

Bill Babbage broke the silence. "Well, Mr Fox," he said, trying to look severe. "You know why we are here. My colleague, Mr Nutter, visited your school a fortnight ago and found many things wrong. But I have to say that, on first impressions at least, it looks as if you have put right a great number of the problems he mentioned."

"Problems?" said Mr Fox, feigning puzzlement. "I wasn't aware of any problems. Nothing has changed since Mr Nutter was last here, I can assure you." Unable to resist twisting the knife in Clive Nutter's wounds, he even added, lying outrageously, "The science block has been up since the beginning of term. A wonderful achievement. Donated by a group of our old boys and girls. Gratitude to the old school. Of course, they can afford it," he added, with a deprecating laugh. "Pupils who leave here seem to have an uncanny knack of landing extraordinarily well-paid jobs!"

"I'm not surprised," said Bill Babbage, "if what I have seen so far of your pupils is an example."

"First, let me show you a copy of our new brochure that one of our pupils has just this moment finished designing. Just a little example of our desk-top publishing course," said Mr Fox. Then he called out, "Asquith Minor!"

The boy entered immediately, carrying a glossy booklet entitled *Burlap Hall – School of the Future*. Bill Babbage turned over the pages admiringly. "Excellently laid-out!" he murmured. "And packed with interesting information," he added. "Very professional indeed."

"Too professional," said Clive Nutter staring over his boss's shoulder. But he was quelled by a look from Bill Babbage.

"Perhaps you'd like a tour of the grounds before we start on the classrooms?" said Mr Fox. "I'd love to show you the science block. It's our pride and joy."

On the way they passed a couple of boys in green aprons, busy grafting one rose on to another. "We're creating a new bloom," explained one boy. "Perhaps we could have permission to name it after you, Mr Babbage?"

"By all means," said Bill Babbage, astonished.

As he spoke, a class of children ran past at enormous speed before pole-vaulting over a seven-foot wall.

"Isn't that rather dangerous?" said Clive Nutter, fumbling for the familiar notebook.

"Dangerous?" said Mr Fox. "Certainly not. They're just limbering up. They do that every morning."

The science block lived up to every expectation. Test-tubes bubbled, germs and viruses lay trapped on glass trays and, when asked what one group was doing, a child answered, through a gauze mask, that they were trying to find a cure for cancer.

"Hardly likely, of course," said Mr Fox, worried that his pupils' exceptional intelligence might be grounds for suspicion. "But we like to encourage them to aim high. And this group, here," he added, pointing to another cluster of students, "is learning how to send a rocket into space."

"I hope they've got permission from the airport authorities," said Clive Nutter, sarcastically.

"Oh, we don't need that!" said Mr Fox, chuckling. "As you see," he added, pointing to another room, "we have our own space simulator on the premises."

Back at the school a pupil helped the visitors off with their coats before ushering them in to a geography lesson. This time, when Mr Roy asked Tom how rocks were formed he was treated to a quarter of an hour lecture. When Mr Roy hurried him up at the end, Tom looked at his watch and said, "Oh! *Latut me tam sero esse!* Oh, I'm sorry," he added, apologetically to Babbage and Nutter. "I'm trying to practise my Latin in every bit of spare time I have. I was looking at my watch and saying I didn't realize how late it was."

Mr Fox was beside himself with glee as he ushered his guests from the school at three o'clock. Bill Babbage had been too embarrassed to stay longer. He was already more than convinced it was the best school he had ever visited in a lifetime of school-inspecting.

"I can't tell you how sorry I am to have put you to the trouble of a second inspection," he said to Mr Fox as he shook hands to say goodbye. "I really can't imagine what my colleague was thinking." He glared at Clive Nutter who stared balefully at Mr Fox. Some trick had been played on him, he was certain. But just what it was, he could not figure out.

As they drove away in their now perfectly-tuned car, the inspector tried a last resort.

"You don't think they were, er, *too* clever?" he suggested.

"*Too clever!*" Bill Babbage exploded with all the rage and fury he'd felt throughout the entire day. "What do you mean, too clever! How can you be too clever! Never have I ever seen a school that impressed me more! Never in my life have I been so ashamed to make a visit as a result of your preposterous report! Never have I been so embarrassed! A hologram! You actually thought the science block was a hologram! And you say you consider St Beowulf's a superior school? Why, it's a museum-piece compared with Burlap Hall! Quite honestly, Clive, I think you ought to look seriously at your future in this profession. Are you sure that a job as a school caretaker wouldn't suit you a bit better? If, that is, you could find a school that would take you!"

Clive Nutter's face twisted into a knot of fury and misery. His yellowing skin grew yellower and yellower and his mouth narrower and narrower. He had been made a complete fool by that wretch, Mr Fox. He would never be able to hold his head high again.

"I'm sorry," he mumbled, bitterly.

"SORRY!" shouted Bill Babbage. And with that they disappeared down the road to Lanchester.

Of course all the pupils' intelligence and politeness wore off at four o'clock and everything got back to normal – except that the school was so much more comfortable and as a result the teachers much more amiable. Burlap Hall suddenly seemed a nicer place to be. As Miles and Tom and Susan were strolling through the science block that Sunday, Tom said, "I know the spaceboys were awful, but in the end everything turned out OK, didn't it?"

"It certainly did," said Miles. "My bed here's even more comfortable than my bed at home."

"Did you hear that since the science block got built Mr Fox has been just inundated with requests from parents dying to send their children here?" said Tom.

"Yes, Burlap Hall's getting to be like Eton. Fox is even going to put up the fees," said Miles.

They wandered through the rooms, marvelling at the equipment, the gleaming instruments, the chemicals, the laser beams, the microscopes, the space simulator. It was all completely incredible.

Then Susan stopped. "What's that?" she said, pointing. On one of the desks a computer had flickered into life. They moved over to have a look. Words appeared on the screen.

"Sorry about the trouble," they read. "Having a great time on Er now our claws have been clipped. Good luck!"

Tom grinned. He typed in, "And good luck to you, too!" Then the screen went blank. The children turned to each other and, smiling, sighed with relief.

Meanwhile, Alf the builder was lying at home in bed. He was completely knackered. He and Bill and Fred had worked harder in the last week than they'd ever worked in their lives. How they'd constructed that science block heaven only knew. The days had passed in a blur of activity and his muscles were aching. Not that he minded very much because now, as opposed to before, he actually *had* muscles, and his shoulders and forearms rippled with bursting brawn.

But finally they had finished; he could have a lie-in at last. His wife had brought him breakfast in bed – and the Sunday paper.

He turned the pages. Usual stuff, he thought. Half-naked girls, pop stars in sex scandals, sportsmen brought low by drugs, drug-takers cured by getting hooked on sport, couples winning thousands on the pools. Then his eye was caught by an odd story.

"'Ace-brain aliens pose problem for posh pupils!'" he read. Underneath was a photograph of the most ridiculous pair he'd ever seen. The man was wearing a dress, and the woman was wearing a suit. They appeared to be stepping out of a flying saucer. An obvious fake, of course. He glanced at the story briefly and then turned over, looking for the sports pages.

Honestly, he thought. These Sunday newspapers! Whatever would they think of next!

VAMPIRE MASTER OF BURLAP HALL
Virginia Ironside

A Burlap Hall Mystery

Is the new teacher a vampire?

There's something very sinister about Burlap Hall's new biology master, Mr A. Culard. He hates light, loves bats and eats dead flies! Now the other teachers are starting to behave oddly too. The question is: will young Tom and his friends, Susan and Miles, get their teeth into the problem before it gets its teeth into them?

"Entertaining... Hilarious moments."
The Junior Bookshelf

PHANTOM OF BURLAP HALL
Virginia Ironside

A Burlap Hall Mystery

Who's haunting the headmaster?

When Mr Fox, Burlap Hall's headmaster, receives a smelly parchment note calling him an "imposter" and signed "The Phantom", he dismisses it as a practical joke. But a series of disasters suggests that the Phantom is both real and deadly serious. Can Tom and his friends, Susan and Miles, come to the school's rescue in this spine-tickling adventure?

POLTERGEIST OF BURLAP HALL
Virginia Ironside

A Burlap Hall Mystery

What is the secret of the restless spirit?

The arrival of menacing Ron Grunt as the new caretaker at Burlap Hall triggers some very weird and destructive events – windows smash, doors break and objects take on a life of their own. A supernatural force is clearly at work... Tom and his friends, Susan and Miles, are soon on the case – and solve a murder too – in this high-spirited adventure!

THE GHOSTS OF RAVENS CRAG
Hugh Scott

It begins on the motorway. The Smiths – Mum and Dad, Sammy, Miff (the narrator) and baby Bertie – are on their way to the Lake District, when they pass an old man in a brown suit, standing on the verge, smiling...

Then on the slip road, they pass him again ... and again... On arrival at their holiday destination, *The Ravens Crag Hotel*, the Smiths soon find themselves drawn into a dark supernatural mystery, involving a boxed-in pew at the local church, a Devil-worshipping child-murderer and the ghosts of dead children. And to be drawn in is to be in danger. Deadly danger...

"Horror and good writing don't often go hand in hand – Scott is a master of the genre."
The Sunday Telegraph

THE PLACE BETWEEN
Hugh Scott

"Don't you know The Place Between? That's what I call it… In the darkness, there is somewhere else that comes between me and this world."

Waking late at night, Stella discovers her friend Daniel at her door, terrified, pleading to be let in. The fearful scratching sounds that follow give credence to his tale of haunted woods and creepy scrabbling twigs. Events quickly become even more sinister and dramatic, until there seems to be only one conclusion: some weird supernatural power is at work. A power that threatens to consume anyone in its path…

"Hugh Scott is a master of the genre."
The Sunday Telegraph

WHY WEEPS THE BROGAN?
Hugh Scott

WED. 4 YEARS 81 DAYS FROM HOSTILITIES

…so reads the date on the clock in CENTRAL HALL. For Saxon and Gilbert it's just another day in their ritualized existence. Saxon bakes, Gilbert brushes, together they visit the irradiated food store, guarding against spiders. Among the dusty display cases, though, a far more disturbing creature lurks. But what *is* the Brogan? And why does it weep?

"Incredibly creepy."
BBC Radio's Treasure Islands

"Very compelling … very interesting."
Jill Paton Walsh,
The Times Educational Supplement

"A new reading experience … a remarkable book." *Margaret Meek, The School Librarian*

Winner of the Whitbread
Children's Novel Award

Shortlisted for the McVitie's Prize

THE HAUNTED SAND
Hugh Scott

"Murder, Frisby!
Murder on the beach!"

There's something creepy in the churchyard.
There's something deathly down on the sand.
Darren feels it, Frisby hears it, George thinks
it's a bit of a laugh. But there's nothing funny
about murder...

"Intriguing ingredients abound: a haunted
church; fearful chases; ghostly weeping; skulls;
bronze helmets; gems and the Black Death...
Rendellesque subtleties of storyline build to an
unforseen climax."
The Times Educational Supplement

"An unmissable book." *Books for Keeps*

GRANNY
Anthony Horowitz

"He could see it in the wicked glimmer in her eyes, in the half-turned corner of her mouth. And it was so strong, so horrible that he shivered. She was *evil*."

Twelve-year-old Joe Warden isn't happy. He has rich, uncaring parents and a granny, who is not only physically repulsive, but horribly mean. She has the look of a predatory crocodile and Joe suspects that she has unpleasant designs on him!

"A hugely entertaining novel."
The Sunday Telegraph

"Anthony Horowitz has created a scary and unmissable old hag." *The Sunday Times*

GROOSHAM GRANGE
Anthony Horowitz

"There's something nasty going on at Groosham Grange…"

Sent to Groosham Grange as a last resort by his parents, David Eliot quickly discovers that his new school is a very weird place indeed. New pupils are made to sign their names in blood; the French teacher disappears every full moon; the headmaster keeps something very chilling in his room… What is the meaning of the rings everyone wears? Where do the other pupils vanish to at night? Most important of all, how on earth can David get away – alive?

This Lancashire Children's Book of the Year will have you gripped and grinning to the last page.

GRIDZBI SPUDVETCH!
Mark Haddon

"It is very simple," he explained, moving his finger along the table. "You have a choice. You can … behave. Or you can … shall we say, face the consequences."

Nine-year-old Jimbo gets into his fair share of scrapes – but nothing to compare with the adventure he and his mate Charlie find themselves in when they plant a walkie-talkie in the staff room. They overhear two of their teachers speaking a weird language. Deciding to investigate, the two boys become caught up in dangerous and thrilling events that are quite literally out of this world!

"Combines spirited social realism with science fiction." *The Independent on Sunday*

GILRAY'S GHOST
John Gordon

"One of your pupils is dead and another, I think, is in danger."

"What kind of danger?"

"Great danger. A ghost doth yearn to take her life away."

In a tomb in the forest, lies the body of evil necromancer Doctor Septimus Carr, whose grisly experiments claimed the life of a servant girl.

Now, two centuries later, another girl is in mortal danger. Enter Gilray. This quirky time traveller has flown back to prevent the looming wickedness. But it's no simple task. For a start, who is the girl – Linda Blake, Pauline Withers, Cassandra Ashe…? Their teacher – flirtatious Bob Wheatley – is the man whose help Gilray needs the most, but he's preoccupied with passionate affairs of his own. Meanwhile, the sinister Rosa and Robin Underleaf are planning to resurrect their "Master"…

Thrilling, intricate, highly entertaining, this tale of horror and desire builds to an intense and chilling climax.